THE GROUNDED GOALIE

ZAC MARKS

"I don't want to be remembered as a good goalkeeper.

I want to be remembered as a great person."

Iker Casillas

1. MISSING

'Where is he?' says Dave, hugging himself to keep warm.

I can't answer. None of us can. No-one knows what's happened to Miles, and the game is about to start.

'If he doesn't show up soon, someone else will have to go in goal,' points out Rex, sounding worried.

It's a grey, overcast day and a light drizzle has started to fall. We're all desperate to get moving; no-one wants to stand around.

I glance at the pitch. It's in a state as usual, more mud than grass, even near the centre. A large puddle stretches from one side of the goal to the other.

'There's no way I'm diving in that.' Brandon folds his arms, daring us to contradict him.

We're all thinking the same. But if Miles doesn't show, one of us is going to get stupidly muddy.

Our coach—Sergeant Brillin—walks over. He's holding his phone. 'I'm afraid I have some bad news. Miles isn't able to play today.'

'Why not?' I ask. 'Is he injured?'

Sergeant Brillin looks flustered. 'I... err... I'm not sure, Jed... Let's not worry about Miles right now. We need to figure out who's going in goal.'

'Shotgun not me,' I say.

'You can't shotgun that!' says Dave. 'We need a fair way to decide.'

'What do you suggest?' asks Luke.

Dave always knows what to do. 'We all write our names on slips of paper. Then choose one at random.'

Brandon shrugs. 'Sounds alright.'

Dave jogs off to find some paper and a pen. The rain is getting worse. We're all thoroughly miserable by the time he gets back.

'Ok, let's get this over with,' mutters Rex.

Dave crouches down and scribbles out our names. He tears the paper into pieces, folding each one up small. He gathers them into his hands and stands up. 'Whoever has their name pulled out, they're in goal, ok?'

We nod, wondering who's going to suffer.

'Rex, you can pick.' Dave holds out his cupped hands.

Rex reaches forward and pulls out a slip. He unfolds it and I see him relax. It's clearly not him.

'Well, who is it?' says Luke, desperate to find out.

'Brandon.' Rex holds up the paper to show us.

'No way!' Brandon pulls a face and runs his hand through his hair. He turns and looks at the goal, then makes a noise of disgust.

'Afraid so. Fair's fair. You got picked.' Dave won't take no for an answer. 'Suck it up, rich boy.'

There's some good-natured banter as we all slap Brandon on the back and wish him luck. He looks like a kid who's about to visit the dentist.

'There are some spare goalie gloves in my dad's coaching bag,' says Luke.

'You need to change your top,' points out Rex, 'or put something over that shirt.'

'I'll grab my sweatshirt. At least it'll keep me warm.' Brandon jogs over to our pile of stuff and comes back with a brand-new drill top and some tatty gloves.

Meanwhile, Sergeant Brillin is chatting with the referee, explaining the reason for the delay.

The field is as bad as ever. The grass squelches underfoot and within minutes of the ref blowing the whistle, we're all spattered with mud. We have the worst pitch in the league. We probably have the worst pitch in the country. But I can't think about that. Right now, I have to focus.

The Brookland Beavers might sound like a terrible football team, but they're surprisingly good on the pitch.

We get a few quick attempts on goal, and things seem hopeful, but the defence soon sharpen up and close us down, making it hard to score. We can win this, but it's not going to be easy.

They soon get in a shot of their own, slicing the ball towards the bottom corner. Brandon hesitates, then dives. He's too late and the ball ends up in the net.

He climbs to his feet, his side plastered with mud. As he wipes his dirty gloves on his shirt, Dave jogs over to him. 'You need to react faster than that!'

'You try diving in this!' complains Brandon.

'I know it's tough,' agrees Dave, 'but let's face it, you're gonna be covered by the end of the match, so there's no point hesitating every time they take a shot. Brave it out like Miles would.'

'I have no idea how he does this every week,' says Brandon darkly. But he takes his place back in the goalmouth.

'This isn't going to go well,' mutters Dave as he jogs back up the pitch towards me. 'Brandon's a useless keeper.'

It's true. Brandon always plays up front. He doesn't enjoy being anywhere else on the pitch. He complains if he has to take a turn in goal.

'Best we can do is make sure they don't get too many

shots,' I suggest. 'Then they can't score.'

It turns out that's easier said than done. In every game, both teams get *some* shots on goal. And if you have a terrible keeper, you soon pay the price. By the time the Beavers have scored their third, I'm beginning to realise how much we take Miles for granted.

Brandon is so muddy it's not even funny. He's been trying, I'll give him that. It's not really his fault. He's a great striker but a shocking goalie.

Sergeant Brillin has come to the same conclusion. He beckons me over.

'What's up, Coach?' I ask.

'Look, Jed, it's three-nil already, and it's not even half-time. If we leave Brandon in the net, then we're going to lose this match by double-digits. I need you to take his place.'

'Why me?' I feel my stomach tighten at the unfairness of it.

'Honestly?' Sergeant Brillin uses his no-nonsense voice, the one you can't argue with. 'Because, without Miles here, you're the best goalie we have. I've seen you in training. The team need you. What do you say?'

I groan. 'Do I have a choice?'

'Not if you want the Foxes to win.'

I'm silent for a moment, weighing up my options.

‘Fine. I’ll do it. But just this once.’ I jog over to where Brandon is standing, shivering in the wind. ‘I’m going in goal,’ I say, unable to keep the annoyance out of my voice. ‘Apparently you suck so bad that I have to take over.’

Brandon shrugs. He’s not offended. ‘Here, you’ll need these.’ He tugs off the gloves and drill top and throws them at me.

‘Gee, thanks so much.’ All the stuff is wet and slimy, and I have to force myself to tug the shirt over my head. Then I strap on the gloves and step forward into the puddle, the only place I can stand if I want to have any hope of defending the net. My nice boots aren’t going to keep my feet dry today; wet mud oozes over the sides. Even though I’m wearing two pairs of football socks, I feel it soaking through.

And the worst part is I’ll have to dive in it.

It’s only a matter of minutes before the opposition take another shot. By now, they’ve worked it out. They’re aiming for the bottom left corner, which is grim, knowing that no goalie is going to be keen to land in that.

But unlike Brandon, I don’t hesitate. I spring to the side like a cat hunting a mouse, the tips of my fingers deflecting the ball around the post. Then I feel it, freezing-cold muck soaking through my kit and splashing on my face. As I scramble to my feet, I realise how terrible this is going to be.

If we're gonna have any chance of winning, I'm gonna be rolling around in it for the rest of the match.

'Thanks, Miles,' I mutter under my breath, trying to wipe my face and only making it worse. 'Thanks a lot. You'd better have a decent excuse for not being here.'

But what if he's injured? What if he can't play for months?

There's no way I'm doing this again.

I need to get to the bottom of this, and fast. The Foxes need their goalie back.

And I need a hot shower.

The sooner, the better.

2. BROKEN

I trudge home, squelching like the swamp thing.

I probably look like a monster, too. Our pitch is always muddy, but I've never been this dirty. There's no part of me that's not covered in muck.

It was worth it, though; they didn't get any more goals. We scored a few ourselves and scraped through with a draw. Nothing like the thumping we'd have got and the fifteen goals we'd have conceded if we'd left Brandon in the net. Luckily, mum will still be at work when I get in so I can sort myself out before she sees how muddy I am.

I head through the gate, shivering in the wind. Our back garden is overlooked by the houses on either side, but I don't care. I kick off my boots and strip off my kit—all of it—right down to my boxers, which are also soaking wet.

Then I unlock the back door and head inside, bundling the filthy kit straight into the washing machine. I pour some powder in the drawer and press the button so it whirs into life.

I used to be annoyed that mum made me do my own washing after football, but today I'm glad. At least I won't get into trouble for the state I'm in. I grin as I think about Brandon. His mum will go ballistic. She hates him getting dirty.

As soon as I step into the shower, I feel better. The water turns brown as it runs through my hair and off my body, but soon I'm warm and clean. We're out of shampoo, so I use the shower gel to wash my hair.

I never want to get that muddy again.

Miles does it every week, even in training. But he's weird like that; he loves mud. Almost as much as he loves getting new goalie gloves.

What's happened to him and why didn't he show?

We tried to call him after the match. Well, Dave did. I never have any credit. But he didn't pick up. It's not like him to let us down.

I don't want the shower to end, but if I use all the hot water, mum will throw a hissy fit. Reluctantly, I turn it off and step out.

I shuffle into my bedroom and pull my thickest clothes out of the wardrobe. I might have warmed up, but the memory of that puddle makes me shiver. Besides, we don't turn the heating on at home unless it's freezing.

That way we save money. If you want to stay warm at my place, you wear lots of layers.

Feeling much more human, I pad downstairs.

BANG! BANG! BANG!

I nearly jump out of my skin. Something bad is happening in the kitchen. It sounds like someone is hammering on the back door or knocking down one of our walls. What if they're trying to get in?

I tell myself not to panic and creep forward to peer through the crack in the door. Now I'm closer, I can tell where the sound is coming from. The washing machine. Something is very wrong. Instead of spinning, it's making weird noises.

I head through and take a closer look. The fast-wash programme is ending, so I should be able to take my stuff out soon, but it's full of water.

Dirty water.

This is not good.

As soon as I can, I open the door. But I wish I hadn't. Muddy water gushes all over the kitchen floor, soaking into my socks; the second time today that my feet have got drenched.

I curse as I reach inside and drag out my Foxes kit. It's still dirty and sopping wet. I don't know what to do with it so I throw it back in the machine. Then I try to mop up the worst of the mess before mum gets back.

It's not easy. The mop just seems to push the filthy water around. Mum arrives as I finish squeezing the last of the water into the bucket.

'Hey kiddo,' she says, bustling through the door. She looks confused as she glances at the kitchen floor. 'Are you doing some cleaning for a change?'

'I had to,' I shrug. 'The washing machine packed in. Water went everywhere.'

Mum groans and heads over. She roots around inside, pulling out my football shirt. 'Well, this amount of mud wouldn't have helped!'

'Sorry. Can we get it fixed?'

She sighs and stands back up. 'We can't afford it.'

'But I need clean clothes!' I blurt out. 'I need my kit for next week!'

'You can wash it by hand,' says Mum. 'That's what we'll have to do with all our clothes until I can find out what it'll cost to repair.'

'Seriously?' I look at her as if she's gone crazy. 'By hand? This isn't the nineteenth century!'

She laughs, despite the stress. 'I'll show you how to do it. Maybe it will teach you to think twice before getting *that* muddy again.'

'It wasn't my fault. Coach made me play in goal. And

you know what our pitch is like.'

Mum looks surprised. 'What happened to Miles?'

'He didn't turn up. We don't know why.'

Mum runs some hot water into a bowl and adds some washing powder. 'Come here, and grab that filthy kit out of the machine.'

I shuffle over and do as I'm told. She shows me how to soak the kit to get the mud out. Cleaning my boots is bad enough. If I have to do this every time I play, then it's going to take hours.

My phone rings, giving me an excuse to step away from the sink. It's Dave.

'Hey Jed, what you up to at the moment?'

I'm too embarrassed to tell him. 'Nothing. Why?'

'Miles still isn't answering his phone, so I'm planning to head over to his place to find out what's going on.'

'But we'll see him in school on Monday,' I point out. 'We can ask him then.'

'Maybe,' agrees Dave. 'But don't you want answers before that? The Foxes need a goalie. What if it's something serious?'

Dave has a point. I won't sleep tonight unless I know Miles is going to make it to our next game. Besides, the Foxes are meant to be a family. Still, something makes me hesitate.

'Doesn't he live in Thelham?' I ask. 'That's miles away.'

'Only three,' he says, as if that doesn't count. 'We can bike there.'

I glance out of the window. It's stopped raining, but it looks cold and miserable. A long bike ride is hardly appealing. But then again... Mum is standing by the sink wringing out one of my wet, muddy football socks. If I stay here, I know what I'm going to end up doing. Anything has to be better than that.

'Mum,' I say, 'Dave wants me to go with him to check on Miles. Can I go?'

'Sure, I guess so. As long as you're back for dinner.'

'I will be. Thanks.' I turn back to the phone. 'Mum says it's ok. Shall I head to your place?'

'Sounds good,' he says. 'See you soon.'

3. GROUNDED

'Here he is!' says Dave, as he opens the front door. 'Our new goalie!'

'It's not funny. I can still taste mud.'

'But you played so well, Jed! You saved us!' Dave's always so upbeat, it's hard to resist his charm.

'Don't get used to it,' I say sulkily. 'I'm not doing it again.'

'Let's hope not. I'll head round the back and grab my bike. You wait here.'

A few minutes later, he emerges through the garden gate and we set off to Thelham.

'I always knew our penalties in the park would pay off,' he says. 'You have great reactions.'

'Yeah, well, just because I'm good in goal doesn't mean that's where I want to play.'

'Don't worry. I'm sure Miles is just sick or something.'

I hope so.

'How do you know where he lives?' I ask after a brief

pause. I realise I've never been to Miles' house before.

'Dad's dropped him home a few times.'

That sounded like something Mr Hughes would do, even though it meant driving all the way to another village. He's nice like that.

'Shame he couldn't give us a lift today,' I mutter as we ride along the wet road.

'He's working,' replied Dave, 'else I expect he would.'

Normally, after I've played football, I'm too tired to bike any distance, but today I've only been standing in the goal, so it's easy. Besides, chatting to Dave keeps my mind off it. We're soon riding past the sign that tells us we're in Thelham.

I follow Dave as he skids around a corner. Thelham's the sort of village where every house is different. He stops by a large cottage. It appears quaint, but was probably built recently. Leaving his bike in the driveway, he approaches the front door.

Dave is one of the most confident people I know. He doesn't seem nervous as he rings the bell, even though he's never spoken to Miles' parents before. But even he's taken aback when a fierce-looking old lady answers.

'Yes? Can I help you?'

'Err, maybe.' Dave's voice falters. I can tell he's wondering if he's got the wrong house. 'Does Miles live here? We play football with him.'

'Oh, do you now?' The lady crosses her arms and scowls at him. 'So, you're the troublemakers, are you?'

'No,' replies Dave. 'We just wondered why he missed the match today. Is he ok? Can we see him?'

'The cheek of it! After everything you've done! How dare you! If I had my way, you'd never see Miles again! Get lost, the pair of you. And don't come back!' She slams the door. Hard.

Dave turns around to me and shrugs, confusion etched across his face. 'What was *that* about?'

I'm as shocked as he is. 'No idea. Someone's got their wires crossed.'

'So, what do we do?' he says.

'Nothing we can do,' I reply, 'except wait until we see Miles at school.'

Dave appears troubled. 'Do you think she meant what she said? About us never seeing Miles again?'

I stare back at him, the implications sinking in. If Miles isn't allowed to see us, he won't be playing football. 'She can't mean that. We haven't done anything. Who is she, anyway? She's too old to be his mum!'

There's a faint knocking sound and I glance up. Miles has his face pressed against his bedroom window and is gesturing to us.

'Look!' I point up at the window.

Two seconds later, Miles holds up a piece of paper. Two words are written on it in big, bold letters: WAIT THERE.

Dave and I hover by the end of his driveway, worried that the old lady is going to come back out and chase us away. But we've biked all this way and we're not going home without answers.

A minute later, Miles reappears. His bedroom window only opens at the top, but he reaches out, his hand holding a paper aeroplane. He tries to throw it to us, but the wind catches it and sends it spinning into a bush at the edge of the lawn.

'He's written us a note,' says Dave. 'We have to get it.'

The bush is right by the front window of the cottage and the plane is stuck in the branches. 'Shotgun not me,' I say, quickly.

'Again, not something you can shotgun!' says Dave firmly. 'Rock, paper, scissors?'

'Ok, fine.'

We bunch up our fists and play a quick round. I lose, as always.

'Unlucky, Jed. I'm sure you'll be fine.'

'Thanks,' I say, glumly.

There's no point trying to creep up to the bush. It's

broad daylight, and that's only going to make me look more suspicious. Instead, I jog over and push my way through the branches, reaching for the paper.

It falls down as I try to grasp it, and I force myself further in. I'm getting scratched all over. I manage to grab hold of the edge of the note and pull it out, stepping backwards onto the lawn. But then I nearly die with fright as someone clutches at my shoulder.

'I TOLD YOU BOYS TO GET LOST!' The old lady is standing right behind me, shouting in my ear, her gnarly fingers gripping my tracksuit top.

'Sorry, we were just...' I realise that if I tell her about the note, then I might get Miles into trouble. But I can't think of any other reason I'd be messing about in her hedge. 'We're going, ok? Right now!'

I pull free from her grasp, run over, and grab my bike. Dave and I pedal off at top speed as the lady shouts after us. 'IF YOU EVER COME BACK HERE, I'M CALLING THE POLICE!'

As soon as we've gone a safe distance, we collapse in a bus shelter.

'I thought I was a dead boy,' I say, panting. 'When I saw her standing there, I nearly wet myself.'

Dave laughs. 'Your face was a picture! I wish I'd filmed it!'

'Yeah, well thanks for being such a good lookout.'

Now he looks embarrassed. 'Sorry. I didn't know what to say. I kind of froze on the spot. She looked so angry.'

'She was crazy,' I agree. 'And she didn't want us anywhere near Miles, that's for sure.'

'But why?' says Dave. 'What did we do?'

'I dunno, but maybe this will give us some answers.' I hold up the tatty paper aeroplane. We unfold it and glance down at Miles' untidy scrawl. 'Sorry I missed the game. I'm grounded. Gran won't let me out. Don't know for how long.'

'Is that it?' asks Dave. 'I was hoping for more than that!'

'Me too,' I agree.

'Well, let's hope we can get some sense out of him on Monday,' grumbles Dave. I note that even he's not sounding optimistic now.

We're much quieter as we ride back to Ferndale.

Why does Miles' gran hate us so much?

And why is he grounded?

And who's going to play in goal for the Foxes?

The thing is, if Miles isn't allowed out, then I know the answer to the last question. It'll be me, for most of the time at least.

I shudder. Whatever's going on, we have to sort it, or

I'm gonna be wet and cold and dirty for the entire season.

It doesn't bear thinking about.

4. BAD

Thick clouds cover the sky, threatening rain.

Perhaps that's why I feel so glum as Dave, Luke, and I wait by the school gates for Miles to arrive.

We see his bus pulling up, and students file off. They push past us, a flurry of coats and bags. But there's no sign of him.

'Where is he?' says Dave, his frustration getting the better of him.

'Dunno,' admits Luke. 'Maybe he missed the bus?'

Then, we see him. He slouches towards the school, scuffing his feet on the pavement.

'Hey, Miles!'

He looks up and sees us. 'Oh, hi.'

'What's happening?' I say, bursting with impatience. 'Why weren't you at the game on Saturday?'

'I got into trouble with my gran.' Miles keeps walking. We fall in next to him.

'It sounds serious,' points out Dave. There's no way

Miles is going to fob us off with some weak excuse like that. 'What did you do? And how long are you grounded for?'

'It's none of your business!' A flash of anger shoots across Miles' face as he turns towards Dave. 'And I don't know when she'll let me come back to football, ok?'

'But we need you,' I whine. 'We've got a game on Saturday.'

'Yeah, sure.' Miles gives me a sharp look. 'You just need me to slide around in the mud because none of you are up for it. Well, I've got other things to worry about.'

'What other things?' Dave looks confused.

'I already told you, it's none of your business!'

Dave turns to me and shrugs. He's all out of ideas.

'We just want some idea of when you'll be back,' I say. 'We miss you, mate.'

'Yeah, I bet. Lose the game, did you?'

Mr Davidson is standing by the door, beckoning us. 'Come on, lads. The bell's about to go! No time to stand around chatting.'

As we slip past, Miles heads off down the corridor to his class. Ours is in the other direction.

'Well, that went well,' mutters Luke.

'This gets weirder and weirder,' says Dave. 'Something is very wrong.'

'Yeah,' I agree. 'And we have to find out what.'

***

At break, we're hoping for another chance to speak with Miles. We're kicking a football around on the playground as usual, but he doesn't show.

'I think Miles might be avoiding us,' mutters Dave.

'Yeah, me too.'

'So, do we let him?' Dave raises his eyebrows.

'No way. Let's find him. He seemed upset. We need to know what's going on.'

'Fine. But he could be anywhere and we don't have long. I'll scout the library and computer room. You check outside.'

'Ok.'

We both slip away from the game. Dave heads inside and I wander round the back of the school, towards the bike sheds. I don't come here often. This is where all the tough kids hang out, laughing and chatting and doing stuff they shouldn't. I try to ignore them as I make my way past.

It's pointless. I won't find Miles here. He's not part of

these groups. He's a good kid; the kind of person who always does his homework on time and who the teachers like. He's probably in the library.

I'm about to turn around and give up when I hear his voice. 'There you go! I did it!'

It's coming from behind the large bins, outside the kitchen. I make my way over and peer around the corner.

I can't believe my eyes.

Miles is standing there, an anxious look on his face. In his hands he has a can of spray-paint. On the wall, he's sprayed 'MJ woz ere.'

There are three others. They all look older than us, even though I know one of them is in our year, a weird kid called Rufus.

'Miles! What's going on?' I say, stepping forward.

Miles spins around. 'Jed, will you please leave me alone? I'm busy.' He turns back to the wall, about to finish his masterpiece.

'No, don't do it!' I reach out and grab the spray-paint from him. 'You're insane! Do you know how much trouble you'll get in?'

His eyes narrow. 'They'll never know it was me.'

'They're your initials, you dummy!' I point at the wall. 'It's hardly going to take a genius to figure it out.'

'That doesn't prove anything.'

'Yeah,' joins in Rufus. 'You tell him, MJ.'

'MJ? What's that? Your new nickname?' I'm furious with him for being so stupid.

He looks away. 'You wouldn't understand. Get lost, Jed.'

'Miles, I...' Words fail me. I don't know how to reason with him. We've played on the same team for years, but it's not like speaking with the same boy. I look down at the can in my hand. 'Please don't do this.'

'Don't do what?' The voice surprises me. It's not Miles speaking, but a man right behind me.

I turn around slowly to find myself face-to-face with Mr Grierson. He's not a teacher you mess with. And he's certainly not a teacher you want to meet when you're holding spray-paint, standing next to a freshly graffitied wall.

'Well, boys, spit it out.' The teacher puts his hands on his hips and stares us down. 'What exactly is going on here, and who is responsible for this... this...' He's struggling to find the words to describe it. 'This act of infantile vandalism!'

We stay quiet. We know the rules. You don't rat on mates, even when you fall out. I glance towards the bins and see that Miles' new friends have disappeared.

'Not in the mood to talk, eh?' Mr Grierson holds out

his hand. 'Give that to me, boy.'

I pass him the can.

'You can both wait outside my office. I'll be in shortly. And at least one of you is going to be very sorry.'

We shuffle off.

'Happy now?' I ask Miles, bitterly.

'No, of course not,' he admits. He looks scared. 'You're not gonna rat on me, are you, Jed?'

'No. But he's bound to find out what happened.'

'Only if you tell him.' Miles gives me a desperate look and for a moment I recognise him as my old teammate. 'If he calls my gran about this, I'll be grounded for even longer. Probably for the whole season.'

'That's not my fault. You should have thought of that before you did it.'

'Maybe. But that's not the point. If that happens, you're going to be without a goalie.'

It takes a moment for that to sink in. If that happens, I know who's going to end up in the net. Basically, if he gets punished, so do I.

'What do you want me to do?' I say.

'Tell him it was you. You were holding the spray paint.'

'Seriously?' I can't believe he's asking.

'Please, Jed. I'll owe you big-time.'

He's giving me a choice. Either I can save his butt and own up to something I didn't do. Or I could find myself stuck in goal for months. It's not a choice I want to make.

I think about it, long and hard. 'Ok, but on one condition. You have to tell me what's going on.'

'I will,' he agrees. 'I promise. Just give me time.'

5. DOOMED

'Well?' Mr Grierson is sitting at his desk, peering at us through his narrow spectacles. 'Is one of you going to tell me what happened, and who's responsible for the graffiti?'

Miles and I are stood in front of him. He hasn't told us we can sit.

It's now or never. There's not much point keeping quiet. Grierson's harsh. If no-one confesses, he'll probably punish us both.

'I was me,' I mutter.

'So, we have a confession.' He leans back and surveys me, a puzzled look on his face. 'But, correct me if I'm wrong; your initials are not MJ, are they?'

'No, sir.' There's no point denying that.

'Whereas yours are?' He glances over at Miles, who shuffles his feet. He couldn't appear more guilty if he tried.

I rush to his rescue. 'I did that deliberately, sir. I wanted to get him into trouble.'

The teacher is silent for a moment while he thinks this through. 'But now you're confessing rather than trying to blame him?'

'You caught me with the spray paint, so I guess you know it was me, anyway.'

He surveys me, still puzzled. 'But when I caught you, you were telling Miles not to do something. What were you telling him not to do?'

'I err, he caught me in the act and was threatening to tell on me. I was asking him not to say anything.'

Mr Grierson gives a curt nod. This seems to make sense to him. 'Well, Miles, it seems you are innocent. I thought it was strange for you to get caught up in something like this. You may go.'

'Thank you, sir.' Miles looks relieved and guilty at the same time. He catches my eye as he leaves the room. *Thank you.*

He better be grateful, because I'm about to go down for what he did.

Once he's gone, Mr Grierson lets out a deep sigh. 'Graffiti, Jed? Really?'

'Sorry, sir.'

'Isn't it a bit, well, childish? Even for you?'

'Yes, sir.'

'So, what are we going to do with you? That is the

question. You realise this kind of vandalism is serious enough to get you suspended?'

I look up at him, fear in my eyes. 'Please don't suspend me. Anything but that. I won't do it again, I promise.'

'Hmmm.' He stares at me for a moment. 'I believe you. And you owned up. There is that.'

Another silence. The wait is killing me.

'So, here's what's going to happen,' he says. 'You're going to spend every lunch time with a bucket of water and a stiff brush, scrubbing that paint off the wall.'

'Yes, sir.' I figure I've got off lightly, all things considered. 'For how long?'

'That's easy,' he replies. 'Until it's clean.'

***

Washing paint off a wall is not easy.

I realise that after scrubbing hard for fifteen minutes and hardly making any difference. I started with hot, soapy water but now it's cold and my hands are numb.

'Jed, I'm so sorry.' I turn to see Miles standing behind me.

'Yeah? Me too.'

'I didn't mean for you to get into trouble. You came along at the wrong moment.'

I scrub furiously at Miles' initials. 'Well, if I hadn't been there, you'd be doing this instead of me. And we wouldn't have a goalie.'

'True.' Miles steps closer. 'That looks hard. Want some help?'

'You better not,' I say. 'If Mr Grierson sees someone helping, I'll get in more trouble. In fact, I'm probably not even meant to be talking to you.'

'Fair enough. I'll go.'

'Wait.' I turn back to him. 'First, you have to explain! Why'd you do it?'

He shrugs. 'It's hard to say.'

'To impress your new friends?'

'I guess,' he admits. 'Sort of.'

'Look, Miles,' I say, getting back to work, 'I can't make you tell me what's going on and it sounds complicated. But we're mates. And the kids you've started hanging around with, they're bad news.'

Miles opens his mouth as if he's going to say something, but we can hear Mr Grierson around the corner, telling some boys to tuck their shirts in.

'I better go.' Miles slips away.

As the teacher arrives, I'm hard at work, though you wouldn't be able to tell. The first two letters have gone kind of smeary, but the wall is a long way from clean.

'Having fun, Jed?' The teacher's lip curls.

'No, sir. This paint is never gonna come off.'

'I'm sure it will eventually,' he says. 'Perhaps next time you'll think twice before defacing school property.'

'Yes, sir.'

He strolls off, whistling.

***

'Every lunchtime?' Brandon looks back at me horrified, his face squeezed between the seats of the bus.

I sigh. 'Yep. Until the wall's clean. But at least Miles didn't get in any more trouble.'

'Not yet, anyway,' mutters Luke, who's sitting next to Brandon. He's kneeling on the seat, facing backwards, so he can join in the conversation.

'What do you mean?'

'Well, if he was stupid enough to graffiti the wall in the first place, who knows what else he's going to do.'

Luke's right, but it isn't reassuring.

'Did any of you get a chance to speak with him?' I ask.

'No,' says Dave, looking glum. 'We looked for him at lunchtime, but he disappeared.'

'We have to find out what's happening. This isn't like him at all. And we need him back on the pitch.'

'True,' agrees Dave. 'But how well do we actually know Miles, when you think about it?'

'He got ninety-six percent on his history test,' says Brandon, as if that told you everything you needed to know about a person.

'But have you ever been to his house?' asks Dave. 'Did anyone know he lived with his gran?'

We give him blank looks.

'He did used to play football with us every lunchtime,' I say. 'And last week he stopped doing that.'

'Maybe something happened to his parents?' suggests Dave, looking troubled.

'Possibly,' I agree. 'But that wouldn't explain why he's hanging around with Rufus and the tough crowd.'

'I asked my dad again when we got back from the match,' says Luke. 'He didn't want to talk about it. I think he knows something but can't say.'

We're quiet for a moment.

'So, what do we do?' asks Brandon, who doesn't like silence.

Even Dave seems stumped. 'I guess we try to speak with him again. Nothing else we can do. We'll hunt him out at break tomorrow.'

I agree. 'The sooner we sort this out, the better.'

But I'm not hopeful. Football training is tomorrow

night, and Miles isn't likely to show.

That's not good news.

Especially for me.

6. ART

The next morning, Miles is in the same art class. It's the best opportunity I'm going to get to speak with him.

Art is one of the few lessons I enjoy at school, other than PE. It's something I'm good at. That's because when I was little, while all the other kids had expensive toys, I played with crayons.

'Hey, Miles,' I say, sitting down next to him.

'Alright?' His expression is impossible to read. I can't tell if he's pleased to see me or if he'd prefer I wasn't there. It doesn't matter; he has some explaining to do.

'Will you make training tonight?' I ask, while the other kids file in.

'Doubt it.' He glances up at me. 'Gran's still mad. I think I'm in for a few more weeks.'

I groan. 'Come on, Miles. Why won't she let you play football? What did you do? You said you'd tell me.'

Miles shifts uncomfortably in his seat. 'It's bad, Jed. I'm in enough trouble as it is. I'm not meant to say.'

The teacher, Miss Elverstone, calls for our attention. 'Good morning, class. How did you all get on with your homework? I hope you have some lovely sketches? I'm looking forward to seeing drawings of the things you love.'

I reach into my rucksack and hunt around for mine, pulling out a sketch of my football boots. When I sit up, Miles is giving me a strange look.

'Jed,' he says, 'I might need to borrow that.'

'Wait? What?' I'm confused.

'Your homework. I need it. I forgot to do mine, and if I get a detention, my gran will go mental.'

'That's your problem.'

'If you were a mate, you'd give it to me,' he says.

'If you were a mate, you wouldn't ask for it,' I shoot back.

'Maybe. But I need it. If I get into trouble, I'll be grounded for longer. Which means...'

He doesn't need to spell it out. We won't have a goalie.

Miss Elverstone is wandering around the classroom, collecting in the sheets. I glance down at my artwork. I spent over an hour on this and I'm proud of it. But we need Miles back on the team more than I need this homework.

I rub my name off the bottom corner and hand it over.

'This is the last time, right?'

'Sure. Thanks!' He scribbles his name.

Miss Elverstone reaches our table and takes the sheet off him. 'This is fantastic, Miles. Much better than your normal stuff.'

'Thanks, miss,' he replies. 'It took me hours.'

'Where's yours, Jed?' she asks, turning to me.

'Sorry, miss, I forgot.' I try to give her my cute look that sometimes gets me out of trouble. 'I was busy with football.'

'Well, that's no excuse.' She's not buying it. 'Stay behind at the end and we'll find time for you to do it one day after school. I'm disappointed in you.'

'Yes, miss. Sorry.'

Not only am I going to get a detention, but she's one of my favourite teachers and I feel as though I've let her down. Worse still, she wants us to work in silence for most of the lesson, so I don't get the chance to grill Miles any further.

When the bell goes, I'm frustrated to see Miles slip away while I have to hold back to chat to Miss Elverstone. I was planning to chase after him but that's not going to happen.

Once everyone else has left, I sidle over to her desk.

'It's not like you to forget your homework, Jed.' The

teacher gives me a meaningful look, like she cares. 'Well, not for art, anyway. I thought this was one of your favourite subjects.'

'It is, miss. I'm sorry. Our washing machine broke, and I got distracted. Things are crazy at home. I'll do it tonight, I promise.' Another of my cute, desperate looks does the trick.

'Ok, Jed, one more chance. I want it handed in before morning registration tomorrow. And it better be good!'

'Thanks so much!' I give her a broad grin. 'It'll be my best work!' I back out of the classroom, relieved that I've escaped.

Well, I might not have a detention but I still have to do the homework again. And that's the second time I've gotten into trouble for Miles already this week.

I'm on my way outside when Mr Davidson, our PE teacher, catches sight of me. 'Ah, Jed! Just the lad I want to see!' He sounds pretty cheerful so I'm guessing I'm not in trouble.

'Hi, sir.' I wait for him to catch up with me. 'What's up?'

'Have you ever considered expanding your sporting prowess, Jed?'

'Sir?' I have no idea what he's on about, and I wish he'd get to the point so I can try to find Miles.

‘Have you thought of trying out any other sports, other than football.’

‘Not really, sir. I love football.’

‘I know that! But I wondered if you’d consider being on the school rugby team as well? We’re short of a few players and you’re fit and you’re fast.’

I point out the obvious issue. ‘I’m also small, sir. They’d crush me.’

‘Not if you’re fast enough,’ grins the teacher, as if he’s made a funny joke. ‘Come on, Jed, you’d be perfect! We have training tomorrow night.’

‘Sorry, sir,’ I say, backing away, ‘but I’m not interested. I’m really busy and rugby isn’t my thing.’

I actually hate it, but I don’t feel the need to say that. He looks disappointed enough as it is.

‘Ok, Jed. Well, if you change your mind, you let me know.’

Yeah, like that’s going to happen.

One thing’s for sure; Mr Davidson will have to find someone else for the team. The last thing I need right now is more time spent sliding around in the mud.

There’s only so much one boy can take.

***

It's freezing.

I don't mean 'cold'. People sometimes say it's freezing when they're wrapped up in warm winter coats and scarves and hats.

They have no idea.

They should try standing on a football pitch in weather like this. It's not even raining, but the wind bites into me and my teeth won't stop chattering. The worst part is, we still have over an hour to go. Practice hasn't even started.

I tug my socks up over my knees and tuck my hands inside my shirt sleeves. I'm wearing the base layers Brandon gave me a few months back, but they're only thin ones, not like the thermals the other lads have.

Sergeant Brillin's battered old hatchback pulls into the car park and Luke jumps out. He shields his face against the wind as he hauls out the bag of coaching equipment and follows his dad to the field.

'Bit of a chilly one today, eh, lads?' says the sergeant.

That's the understatement of the year.

'It's sub-zero!' says Brandon. 'Can't we call it off?'

'No way, son.' Sergeant Brillin shakes his head. 'You might have to play games in these temperatures so you need to practice in them as well.'

That's easy for him to say, but I notice that he's

bought himself a new coat which reaches almost to his knees.

'Still no Miles, then?' asks Luke, looking around.

'It appears not,' mutters Theo.

'Looks like you're in goal again, Jed,' says Rex.

'No way!' I object. 'Not again!'

'But you're our best goalie.'

'I'm not always going in goal, just because Miles isn't here. Someone else can take a turn.'

The lads look at each other awkwardly.

Brandon says what they're all thinking. 'You have to, Jed. You're much better than any of us.'

'It doesn't matter,' I say. 'Besides, it's just a practice.'

'But what's the point in someone else practising in goal if you're the person who plays there?' says Theo. A few others nod.

It feels like they're ganging up on me. 'IT'S FREEZING! I'm not going back in!'

'I'll do it,' offers Dave, keen to stop us arguing. 'I'll be goalie for today. Jed's right. We have to take it in turns.'

Sergeant Brillin clears his throat. 'Well, actually lads, we don't even need a goalie for the drills we're doing, so it's not worth arguing about.'

Everyone looks relieved.

We get stuck in, racing around cones, passing and

tackling each other. Once I'm moving, my body soon warms up. This is where I want to be, out on the pitch.

'We may not need a goalie right now,' puffs Rex, as he dribbles the ball next to me, 'but we're going to need a plan for the game on Saturday.'

Brandon overhears. 'He's right, Jed. We need you to step up.'

'I would, but it's just too cold! You guys at least have winter base layers and stuff. I'll die!'

I hope that will make them back off, but Brandon sees a solution. 'Hey, I'll sort you out mate! I have loads of stuff!'

'Thanks, but you're missing the point! I don't *want* to play in goal!'

Rex pauses and looks me in the eye. 'Neither does anyone else. And you're the best. Take one for the team.'

I clench my fist in frustration. What does Rex think I've been doing this entire time? I want to punch him in the face, but somehow, I hold back.

The thing is, I know how this will end. They'll eventually wear me down, make me feel guilty.

And when they do, I'll end up exactly where I don't want to be. I glance at the puddle between the goalposts and shudder.

This is not good.

7. PHONE

The thing about being a striker is, you know how to zone in on your target.

On Wednesday morning, at the end of our science lesson, I'm not letting Miles out of my sight. As soon as the bell goes, I follow him out of the classroom.

'Where are you off to?' I demand, as he makes his way down the corridor.

'Honestly, Jed, I wish you'd leave me alone.'

'Yeah? You didn't say that when you wanted my homework.'

He stops and sighs. 'Ok, whatever. You can come if you want. I have to get something, but don't blame me if you get into trouble.'

'Why? What are you up to now?'

'One of my mates had their phone taken off them earlier, and I'm gonna get it back.'

'You can't be serious?' I grab his shoulder and try to reason with him. 'You can't go taking stuff out of a teacher's desk.'

'Watch me,' says Miles. 'Real mates do that kind of thing for one another. But I guess you wouldn't know.'

'What are you on about?'

'We've never been mates. Not really. We just play on the same team.'

'That's rubbish, Miles. We've known each other for years.'

'You've never invited me round your house though, have you?'

'I never invite anyone to my place,' I admit. 'It's, err, not that great. I don't have much stuff.'

'Sure, ok. But you, Brandon, Dave and Luke hang around together all the time.'

'Yeah, but...' I trail off.

Now I'm starting to understand. He's feeling left out.

But that's stupid, isn't it?

The more I think about it, the more I realise that we never invite Miles to our sleepovers and gaming sessions. It's not that we don't like him; just that he lives in a different village.

'Look, I'm sorry if we've not always invited you. But that doesn't mean we're not mates.' As I say it, I realise how daft it sounds.

'Whatever.' Miles heads out of the double doors

towards the sports block.

'Seriously, where are you going?'

'Mr Davidson's office. That's who took the phone.'

'And you're planning to snatch it back? Don't you think he'll wonder where it's gone?'

'I've thought about that.' He gives me a sly look.

'Yeah?'

'I'm going to leave my phone instead. Mr Davidson won't know the difference. They're all just shiny black things as far as he's concerned.'

He's probably right, but it's still a stupid thing to do. 'If you get caught, you're gonna be in so much trouble.'

'It's worth it.' He says it stubbornly, daring me to contradict him. 'I'd do anything for one of my mates. But like I say, you wouldn't get that.'

'I would, Miles.'

'Yeah? Then prove it. Help me get this phone back.'

I pull a face. 'It's too risky.'

'Thought as much.' He picks up his pace, trying to leave me behind.

'Fine, I'll do it. Then will you believe that I'm your mate?'

'It's a start.'

I realise that somehow he's done it again. He's persuaded me to do something that could get me into a lot of trouble. But it's too late to back out now. 'What's the plan?'

'I'm hoping that he's left his office open while he's gone to the staff room for coffee.'

'I doubt it.' We're getting close now, right outside the gym.

'Worth a shot, though,' points out Miles. 'I'm going to take a quick look. You wait here.'

'Sure.'

He's back within seconds and there's a problem. 'Mr Davidson is still there. We're gonna need to distract him.'

'How?' I ask. My stomach is tight.

'One of us needs to call him outside. Maybe we could say someone's injured?'

'And when he gets outside and finds no-one's there, what do we do then?' I look at him as if he's stupid. He hasn't thought this through.

Miles isn't put off. 'I have an idea. I'll deal with Mr Davidson. All you have to do is switch the phones.' He hands me his shiny black handset. 'Swap the one in his desk with this one.'

'I dunno, Miles. This is a really bad idea.'

'Are you a mate or aren't you?'

'I am.'

'Then do this one thing for me, ok?'

'Ok.' I want to point out that I've already done more than one thing for him this week but there's no time. He's reaching into his bag and pulling out his water bottle. Then he slips into the empty sports hall.

What is he up to?

I can feel my heart thudding against my chest as I prepare for action. I'm like a coiled spring, waiting to be let loose. A few seconds later, Miles is back in the corridor and this time he knocks on Mr Davidson's door.

The teacher swings it open, irritated at being disturbed during his break. 'Miles, what is it?'

'Sorry to bother you, sir, but there's something weird in the gym. It looks like the roof's leaking. I think you should take a look.'

'I'm sure it's just a spillage.' Mr Davidson follows Miles down to the sports hall, not bothering to lock the door. 'Why on earth were you in there, anyway?'

'I thought I left my watch there,' says Miles. 'I went to look and I saw the puddle.'

As soon as they're out of sight, I jump into action and sprint into the office. It's in a proper state as usual. I nearly trip over the pile of cones that have been dumped near the doorway. Dirty rugby kit is piled in the corner, giving the room a weird smell. On one side of the cramped space is a wooden desk with three drawers. I pull open the top one, hoping to find a phone, but the drawer is as messy as the rest of the room. I have to rummage around amongst random stationery, a few ripped exercise books, a phone charger and some tools. No phone.

I slam the drawer shut and open the next one. A sweaty pair of shin pads sits next to a packed lunch.

That's gross. Why would anyone do that?

Maybe PE teachers all lose their sense of smell, being around kids all the time?

The bottom drawer is full of folders. As I shift them aside, I spot it: a shiny black smartphone. I grab it and replace it with the one in my hand. They're different models, but Miles is right; Mr Davidson isn't likely to notice.

I'm about to leave when I hear voices outside. They're coming back! If I try to leave the office now, I'll be seen. I glance around, frantically looking for somewhere to hide.

For a second, I consider diving underneath the filthy rugby kits, but the handle is already turning, so instead I slump into one of the soft chairs.

'Ok, Miles, thanks for bringing it to my attention.' Mr Davidson opens the door. 'Jed! What are you doing here?'

'Err, I wanted to see you sir.' I try to look innocent. 'Your door was open, so I thought I'd wait here. I hope that's ok?'

The teacher frowns. 'Not really. You don't go into a teacher's office when they're not there.'

'Sorry, sir.' I have to distract him, so he's not suspicious. I blurt something out. 'I just wanted to chat more with you about the rugby team.'

'I thought you weren't interested?'

'You just caught me off-guard. Now I've had time to think about it, I reckon it'd be a laugh. How do I sign up?'

It works. Mr Davidson is no longer concerned about finding me in his office. He's focused on rugby instead. 'Well, Jed, it would be great for you to join. Like I said before, we need some more players. But we practice on Wednesday evenings after school, and we don't cancel if it's raining. Rugby is played in all weathers.'

'I'm up for that.' I shrug as if it's no big deal. 'It'll be fun.'

'Want to join us tonight?'

No chance.

I quickly think up an excuse. 'I'd love to sir, but my mum will expect me home and I don't have my kit.'

'That's not a problem. I'll give your mum a call and check if it's ok. And you can borrow some kit.'

Mr Davidson logs into his computer and pulls up my mum's contact details. As he picks up his phone and types in the number, I glance over at the dirty rugby shirts.

Please don't pick up, please don't pick up.

I hope my mum is busy vacuuming someone's house or has forgotten to charge her phone. But, sadly, she answers. It only takes Mr Davidson a couple of minutes to explain the situation and she's more than happy to give permission.

He hangs up, looking satisfied. 'Your mum's fine with you staying on,' he smiles.

'Great,' I say, my voice strained. 'Thanks, sir.'

'No problem. I'll see you at four o'clock.'

I head out of the office and take a deep breath. That was close. I nearly got caught. Who knows what would have happened if Mr Davidson had caught me fumbling around in his desk?

'You ok?' Miles heads over, looking concerned. 'Did you manage to do it?'

'Yeah. But I also had to join the rugby team, so he wasn't suspicious.'

'You absolute legend!' Miles looks pleased as he takes the phone out of my hand and examines it.

'Are we mates now?'

'Sure.' He looks up at me and smiles. 'If you want?'

'Of course I do.' We bump fists. 'But now you have to tell me what's been going on. Please, Miles?'

'Ok,' he says. 'I'll tell.'

The bell rings and I curse as we hurry towards our next lesson. Miles looks back at me. 'I'll meet up with you at lunch. Perhaps we can chat then?'

'I can't. I have to clean up your artwork, remember?'

'Oh yeah. Why don't I phone you after school?' Miles smacks himself on the forehead. 'Oh wait, I just lost my phone didn't I? It'll have to be tomorrow then.'

There's no time to reply as we're swept along the corridor by students making their way to lessons. He goes one way and I go the other.

And I wonder if I'm ever going to find out what's going on.

8. RUGBY

I walk into the changing rooms, tired and nervous. It's been a long day, and I spent my whole lunch break scrubbing a wall. Right now, I wish I was getting the bus home. Instead, I have rugby training.

Glancing around, I don't feel any better. None of my mates are here. Instead, I'm surrounded by kids who hit puberty way too early. A few of them seem surprised to see me.

'Look who it is!'

Uh-oh. I know that voice.

I turn to the left to find Tristan, my worst enemy, standing there with a sneer on his face. I want to say something but can't find any words.

'Aren't you a bit small to play rugby?' Tristan strolls over, popping his collar up. He's a head taller than me and he comes much too close. 'You realise this is a man's sport?'

'Mr Davidson asked me to.' I try to turn away but

Tristan grabs my shoulder.

'Well, then, welcome to the team.' He gives me an evil grin. 'I just hope you don't find it a little too rough for your liking.' He almost hisses the words. A clear threat.

'I'll be fine.' I try not to sound worried. 'Can't be worse than playing the Welbeck Warriors at football.'

That makes some of the other lads laugh.

'That's what you think.' Tristan returns to the bench and starts pulling on his socks, giving me dark looks.

This isn't good. Tristan has wanted revenge ever since Dave and I made him fill his boots with syrup. He's laid low for ages but he hasn't forgotten what happened. Now I'm on my own, he has the perfect opportunity to get his own back.

'Ah, Jed, there you are.' Mr Davidson strolls into the changing rooms. 'You need a kit, right?'

'Sure.'

What I really need is some time chilling on FIFA, but that's not gonna happen.

'Here you go.' He dumps a pile of stuff on the bench. 'It might be too big for you, but I'm sure you'll manage for today. And get yourself some boots out of lost property.'

'Thanks, sir.'

As soon as he's left, Tristan is back on my case. 'Watch

your boots, lads. Jed might steal them.'

I don't respond but my cheeks burn as a few others snigger.

I pull off my uniform, then pick up the red and yellow hooped rugby shirt. It's still damp, as though someone wore it last lesson, and it smells of sweat. One arm is already covered in mud. But that's not the worst part. This shirt isn't just a bit too big, it looks like a dress on my skinny body. I have to tuck it into the shorts, which are also damp and baggy.

As I pull on the dirty yellow socks, I see Tristan glancing over at me, a smirk on his face. He's already imagining a thousand ways to cause me pain.

How did I get into this?

I want to believe that it's all worthwhile, now that Miles is starting to trust me. But deep down, I have my doubts. He keeps getting away with stuff and I keep paying for it.

And he still hasn't told me what's going on.

I rummage around in the grim box, looking for some boots. Last time I did this, I found a decent pair of Nexus Cheetahs, but this time there's only one pair that will fit me: a cheap, no-brand pair made of shiny black plastic.

As I pull them on, Tristan can't resist another dig. 'New kicks, Jed? They're expensive for you, aren't they?'

Before I can respond, the changing room door opens again and Mr Davidson calls. 'Come on, lads, we haven't got all day. Let's go!'

We file out, our boots clattering on the tiled floor.

A powerful gust of wind batters into me as I step outside, sending a shiver down my spine.

Get it together, Jed. You'll soon warm up.

I break into a jog. The grey sky and steady rain don't improve my mood. Neither does the sight of the field, which is covered with puddles.

Mr Davidson tells us to do a few laps while he lays out some cones. We return, panting a little as we stand and face him.

'Right, for the first drill you need to be in pairs.'

A firm hand grabs my shoulder. It's Tristan. 'I'll team up with you. I don't want you feeling left out.'

I glance around, hoping there's someone else I can go with, but everyone already has a partner.

'What you're going to do,' explains Mr Davidson, 'is simple attack and defence. One of you has the ball and tries to run from one end of your rectangle to the other. The other one tries to stop them by tackling them. If you get to the other side, you score a point. If they take you down, they do. Then you swap over and play again. Got it?'

Everyone nods and grunts. They've done this before. Tristan grabs a ball and gives me a wicked grin. 'Come on, Jed. You're gonna love this.' He jogs over to one rectangle Mr Davidson has marked out with cones, the muddiest one he can find.

'Here!' He throws me the ball, hard. I double over as I catch it against my stomach. 'You go first.'

I'm standing on the line and he's facing me, his legs apart, his head cocked to one side. He can't wait to crush me. There's nothing I can do except try to outrun him.

I sprint forward, feinting and dodging to get past, but within seconds his body is wrapped around my legs and I crash to the ground.

At least it's soft.

'That's one point to me,' he says. 'Now it's my turn.'

He snatches the ball and takes a place at the line. He runs towards me before I've even got to my feet. I lunge towards him as best I can, but he stamps on my hand as he pulls away.

'Arrrrggghhh!' I cry out, rubbing my throbbing fingers.

'You can't go in half-hearted, Jed,' calls out Mr Davidson, cheerfully. 'That's how you end up getting hurt. You have to commit and throw your whole body into it. And your hands should end up near his waist, not his feet.'

'Yes, sir,' I say, annoyed. I've just been stepped on and apparently it's *my* fault.

'That's two to me,' points out Tristan, raising his eyebrows. 'Your turn to run again.'

I take the ball.

At one side of our rectangle there's a muddy puddle, which I'm trying to avoid. But I sprint towards it, planning to switch direction at the last moment.

I'm fast, but the rectangle is tight, and Tristan blocks the space I was hoping to use, forcing me into the slippery corner. I feel his weight crashing into my side, his arms tight around me. Instead of dropping me to the floor, he pulls me around, depositing me right in the centre of the puddle, my face splashing down.

I stagger to my feet, covered in wet mud, my hair lank.

'Three to me,' he says, a thin smile on his face. 'Enjoying your first rugby practice?'

I want to have a go at him, but don't want to give him even more satisfaction. He has me exactly where he wants me, and there's nothing I can do. I clench my jaw and take my place for the next round.

The drill goes on for what feels like forever. He's winning twelve-nil when Mr Davidson calls it to a halt. By then everyone is wet and dirty, but no-one has been hammered as badly as me.

The rest of the practice isn't any better. Tristan uses every drill as an excuse to punish me. By the time we finish, I limp back to the changing rooms, battered and bruised, soaking wet and miserable.

'Same time next week?' says Tristan. He ruffles the back of my wet hair. 'You're gonna so regret what you and your mate did to me.'

He's right.

I already do.

9. HOME

I step off the bus and trudge up the street feeling sorry for myself. I'm wondering how long it will be before I can quit the rugby team. I don't want Mr Davidson to be mad.

Just as I think things can't get any worse, I turn the key in the front door and see a note from mum. 'Jed, hope you had a good day. You need to do some of your washing tonight. Use the sink like I showed you, then hang it on the rack to dry. Love you.'

I curse under my breath as I kick off my shoes. I don't see why I should have to do my washing. None of my mates do. But Mum is working stupidly hard at the moment, cleaning other people's houses. I don't want to cause her more stress.

I head to my room and gather the pile of clothes from the last five days. I've tried to wear the same stuff for as long as possible, but it still seems like a lot. And my Foxes training kit is muddy from our last practice.

Hauling it down to the kitchen, I fill the sink with hot water, and pour in some washing powder. Once it's full, I take a deep breath and plunge in some clothes. I start with the cleaner stuff as my kit will get the water filthy.

Why did the stupid washing machine have to break?

Nothing in my life is ever easy. That's what it's like being poor. I'm used to that. But right now, things are even worse than normal. Maybe I should never have tried to help Miles? Maybe I should have stood my ground and refused to go in goal when the team hassled me? I keep trying to do the right thing but now I'm stuck doing things I hate.

I'm squeezing out one of the school shirts when my phone rings. I reach for it, then realise my hands are dripping wet so I rub them against my trousers first. Today is not going well.

'Hey, Jed!' It's Brandon, sounding way too cheery. I can imagine him kicking back in his massive bedroom on a beanbag with a can of Coke and a chocolate bar, playing FIFA.

'Hi Brandon,' I sigh. 'What's up?'

'We missed you on the bus,' he says. 'Dave said something about you signing up for rugby practice.'

'Yeah, he's right. I did.'

There's a moment of quiet as Brandon digests this.

'No offence, mate, but are you *mental*? You know that Tristan's on the rugby team?'

'I do now,' I say, 'but I had to. It's a long story.'

'Well, why don't you head round?' he says. 'Then you can fill me in and I can give you some goalie stuff before practice tomorrow.'

I glance at the sink, and my muddy kit on the floor. 'Sure. But there's something I need to do here first. I'll be about half an hour.'

'That's good with me. See ya.' He hangs up, returning to his perfect life while I get back to my problems. I shouldn't be mad at him; he's trying to help.

I spend the next twenty minutes plunging and stirring my clothes in the water. I have no idea if I'm doing it right. Getting them dry enough to hang up is the hardest part. I have to properly squeeze them out, but even then they're much wetter than when they come out of the machine. I wish we could afford a tumble dryer, but unless we win the lottery, that's never gonna happen.

I hang them on the rack, where they drip onto the tiled floor. My blue and white training kit doesn't look great; I got out the worst of the mud but it still looks stained and grubby. It's the best I can do. I guess it'll only get wrecked again next time I play.

I write a quick note to mum before I grab my bike and

set off to Brandon's.

It's still raining outside, giving my hair another soaking as I bike the short distance. At least I'm moving, which helps me to stay warm. It's not like that when I have to stand in goal. I wonder if I'll ever get used to it, being cold and wet. Maybe at some point you become immune? Maybe that's how Miles deals with it?

If so, I still have a long way to go.

I cycle up Brandon's long driveway to his massive house. There's a dirty builder's van in the driveway; it looks as out of place as I do, next to the immaculate front garden.

I ring the bell. Brandon doesn't answer of course. That would take too much effort. His mum comes to the door instead. For once, even she looks harassed and distracted. There's the sound of banging and crashing coming from the kitchen.

'Oh, Jed.' She says it like she was expecting someone else.

'Sorry to bother you. Brandon invited me.'

'Yes, of course. Come in.'

I kick off my shoes as I step inside, glad I'm wearing grey socks today so she can't see how dirty they are. But, for once, Brandon's mum isn't interested in the state of my clothes. Instead, she's staring at my face. 'Did you fall off your bike?'

Now it's my turn to look confused. 'No. Why?'

'Your face is covered in mud.'

I'd forgotten about that. I haven't washed since rugby. My hair must look pretty awful too. I'm tempted to make a joke of it and tell her it's not yet time for my monthly shower, but she'll probably think I'm being serious.

'I had rugby practice.'

'Right, well, you know where Brandon's room is. And the bathroom, if you want to, err, well...'

'Yeah, thanks.' I bound up the stairs, glad to get away.

'Hey,' says Brandon, jumping up as I walk in. He's wearing a gleaming white and pink Paris Saint-Germain kit today which looks like he just took it out of the packet. 'You look rough!'

'Thanks. I think your mum agrees.' I smile at him. His mum's dislike of me is a running joke.

'Ignore her. She's stressed at the moment,' he says. 'We're having a new kitchen put in and she can't cope. There's mess and dust everywhere. You should have seen her face when one of the builders used the downstairs loo and didn't exactly hit the target.'

'Ouch. I bet that didn't end well?'

'Nah, she had a right go at them. I don't think they dare use the toilet now!'

That cheers me up. 'Why do you need a new kitchen? Your old one was amazing.'

'Meh, dunno.' Brandon says it like he's given up trying to work out his parents. 'Wasn't the right colour or style or something. Who knows? Anyway, we have more important things to discuss than kitchens!'

'True. You said you've got some goalie stuff?'

Brandon heads over to his floor-to-ceiling wardrobe and slides it open. 'Not just *some* goalie stuff Jed. This stuff is a game-changer. Check this out.' He throws some shiny black items at me.

At first I think it's a fancy dress costume, like when people dress up as Batman or something, but it's actually a set of skins. They're thicker than the ones I have at home and they have padding in the chest, the arms and the legs.

'What is this?' I say, squeezing the material between my fingers.

'It's specialist goalie stuff by Keeper-Tech. They're one of the best companies for protective equipment. Try it on!'

I unbutton my school shirt and let it fall to the floor, then tug on the top. It clings to my body. The pads feel weird, especially on the elbows.

'It's nice, but it doesn't feel that warm,' I comment.

'That's because you've only just put it on, dufus.' Brandon gives me a playful shove. 'Do a couple of press-ups. It'll heat up. You'll see.'

I'm curious enough to try. Sure enough, as soon as my body warms up, so does the top, trapping the heat against my skin.

'It's pretty good,' I admit. 'A lot better than mine.'

'Yeah, well wait until you've got it over your legs as well. You'll be toastie.'

I can't imagine that's true. I mean, I'll be a lot warmer than I was last time I was in goal, but no-one can stand in a puddle for an hour and not feel chilly, whatever they're wearing.

'You don't mind me borrowing these?' I ask. 'They must be expensive.'

'Feel free.' Brandon crashes down on his bean bag. 'You're gonna need them more than I am.'

'True.' I don't need reminding. 'Why do you have this stuff, anyway? You hate playing in goal.'

'My parents bought it for me,' he says. 'Because I kept complaining that I got too cold playing in winter. But it turns out that if you run around all game in that, you have the opposite problem. You get way too hot!'

'You sure you didn't get this so the girls thought you had a six-pack?'

'Right, you're gonna get it for that!' He leaps up and jumps on top of me, wrestling me to the ground.

I laugh and roll over, while he punches me on the arm.

'I can't even feel that,' I point out. 'Not with all this padding!'

'See, I told you it was good!' He gives up and climbs off me, sitting on the bed. 'So, are you gonna tell me why you joined the rugby team? Did you see an advert that they needed a new punchbag and think you'd apply?'

I snort. 'Not exactly. But that is pretty much what I am. Truth is, it's all Miles' fault...'

I tell him the full story of what happened, leaving nothing out.

He lets out a low whistle. 'Miles has properly dropped you in it.'

'Too right! And I still don't know what's happening! We could be without a goalie for months!'

'That's harsh, Jed.' It's rare for Brandon to show concern. He's not that sort of mate. 'You can have the skins for as long as you want. Keep them if you like. How are you stocked for goalkeeper kits?'

'I have the one you gave me before.'

'I can find you another one.'

'That would be awesome. You've already given me too much, though. I'll manage.'

'You sure? You don't want this?' He tugs out a turquoise strip.

'That does look pretty cool,' I admit. 'It's a lot better than the fluorescent yellow and black one I have at home.'

'Take it. We want our goalie looking the part.'

'If you're sure? Thanks, Brandon. You're a mate. I think I'm all set.'

'One more thing!' Brandon rummages around in his wardrobe and pulls out some goalie gloves. 'I think they're better quality than the ones Coach has in his bag.'

'I'd say.' Sergeant Brillin's gloves probably date back to the eighties.

I try them on. They make my hands twice as big.

'I reckon you could save anything with those,' says Brandon.

'Yeah, maybe.'

They'll help me reach further when I dive for the ball, and they have amazing grip.

But there's only one thing I'm really interested in saving right now.

And that's Miles.

10. TRAINING

Brandon's right. The base-layers are a total game-changer. As I pull them on before Thursday night's training session, they hug my body tightly, offering me some level of comfort as I glance out the window at the grey sky.

My training kit is still damp, so I reluctantly grab the luminous yellow goalie kit out of my wardrobe. Brandon gave me this when I needed something bright for my paper round. I never thought I'd need it again, but I want to save the new turquoise strip for the game at the weekend. The shirt and shorts glow like toxic waste in a cartoon and the socks have neon yellow and black hoops. It would be hard to imagine a worse strip.

I know I look stupid, but the padding gives me extra confidence. As I step outside and start riding my bike down to the field, I'm much warmer than before.

Dave raises his eyebrows when he sees me. 'Nice kit,' he teases.

'Shut it.' I throw down my bike and saunter over to

him. 'It's one of Brandon's.'

'There's a surprise.'

'But check this out.' I lift the shirt to show him the padded base layers on my chest.

'You been working out?' he says, then steps out of the way as I aim a punch at his arm.

'You're a funny boy,' I say. 'But this stuff is amazing. I'm gonna be so much warmer today.'

'I'm glad you're feeling positive, because that goal still looks horrendous.'

I glance over. 'It'll be fine.'

Sergeant Brillin calls us. As the team gathers, he turns to me. 'Correct me if I'm wrong, Jed, but you look like you're up for going in goal?'

'If the team need me, I will. No-one else wants to.'

'I'm impressed, lad. That's real teamwork right there!' He looks around. 'Jed here has the right idea. We're going to be thinking hard about teamwork in the coming few weeks, and our attitude to our teammates.'

'Yeah?' says Theo. 'If he cares about us so much, couldn't he have worn something less bright? That stuff hurts my eyes!'

A few lads laugh, but Sergeant Brillin presses on. 'When you've all quite finished taking the mick, you should all say thank you to Jed for being willing to cover for us while Miles is off. I'm sure he'd rather be up front.'

'Too right,' I mutter. 'Do you know how long Miles is gonna be grounded for?'

Sergeant Brillin hesitates. 'I, err, I'm going to meet with his gran soon and see if I can find out when Miles will rejoin us. But before that, we have a game on Saturday. And this Sunday I've arranged a special team-building session for you all.'

Even Luke looks surprised. 'What's that, Dad?'

'It's an opportunity for you to all learn more about the importance of trusting one another and working together.'

'Yeah, but what *is* it?' asks Rex.

'You'll see on Sunday. I'm not going to spoil the surprise. I've texted your parents with the details.'

I'm not sure whether that makes me excited or nervous.

'C-C-Can we get started on training?' asks Ashar. He's freezing, but I've barely noticed the temperature after cycling here in my skins; they really do make a difference.

'Sure. Right, let's get warmed up...' Sergeant Brillin barks out orders. Before long, we're ready to properly get stuck in. 'Ok, lads, today I think we need to give Jed here as much practice as he can get. You up for that, Jed?'

'Sure. Bring it.'

'That's the spirit,' says Sergeant Brillin, pleased. 'Right, you better get in position. We'll start with some attacking and defending drills, then take some corners and penalties.'

I'm not left standing around. The entire session is an onslaught of jumping and diving, slithering and sliding in the mud, saving shots, tackling defenders. That might sound grim, but it's ok. I don't have time to get cold or think about the conditions. Every few seconds there's another challenge, another ball to save.

'I'll get it in next time,' shouts Dave, as I snatch one of his shots out of the air.

'Want a bet?' I hurl the ball back.

'Jed, you're on fire!' says Brandon as I dive to the far corner, sending his shot wide. 'I hope you can play like this on Saturday!'

'Yeah,' I reply, 'so do I.'

Who knows? I think to myself. *Maybe playing in goal isn't so bad after all?*

***

On Friday, another good thing happens.

Well, sort of good anyway.

It's break time at school and I'm sitting on the toilet

when I hear some kids come in. At first, I don't recognise the voices.

'He's such a loser.'

'Are we inviting him to the gaming session tomorrow?'

'His gran won't even let him out. Not after last week. He's only allowed to play online.' I know who this is; it's Rufus.

'Well, at least we don't have to come with excuses why he can't hang out with us.'

'Hey, don't be harsh. He's alright. He did all of my maths homework this week. And he got me a decent mark.'

'True. And he even risked his neck and got my phone back.'

'Yeah, but he's still a loser.' They laugh at this and I feel my anger boiling up. How could they be so cruel? Miles is decent. He doesn't deserve that kind of abuse.

I want to get out there and stick up for him but I'm half-way through my business and my trousers are round my ankles. It wouldn't be a good idea anyway. There are three of them and they're much bigger than me.

'So, we're not telling him about tomorrow?'

'Nah, he'll only ask to connect remotely or something. We'll have to say we're all busy.'

'Besides, he needs time to do my English homework.'

'The whole essay? How did you persuade him to do that?'

'Usual story. Told him a whole sob story about how I struggle with schoolwork and how I'm worried they'll keep me back a year. Stuff like that.'

More laughter.

'Tell you what, I'll invite him to log in tonight for an hour or two, so he doesn't get suspicious. Just don't mention Saturday.'

'Yeah, good plan.'

There's the sound of taps being turned on and paper towel being pulled from the dispenser.

'You know he's gonna catch on eventually, right?'

'I dunno. I reckon he'll do anything to be part of our gang.'

'We'll soon find out.'

With that, they're gone.

And I finally understand what's happening. They're using Miles. His new 'friends' aren't friends at all. They're making him do their homework and take risks for them, all the time pretending that he's one of the crew.

But they have no plan to include him, really.

They're stringing him along.

It's a cruel thing to do and I have to tell Miles.

I finish cleaning up, flush the toilet and wash my

hands at record speed. Then I dash around the school, desperate to find him.

But it's a big school and I only have five minutes.

It turns out, that's not enough.

When I trudge into afternoon registration, I haven't been able to speak with him. He's none the wiser about Rufus and his cronies. And I have no idea when I'll be able to tell him what I heard.

11. PRESSURE

I'm back in the net.

But this time it matters. This time it's for an important game; a match against one of the best teams in the league, the Delton Dynamos.

I'm wearing the special base layers, along with the turquoise goalie kit Brandon gave me and the top-brand gloves. I look pro and I'm feeling confident. If I can play like I did at practice on Thursday, then we're going to be fine.

We're at their pitch. It's muddy, but nowhere near as bad as ours. I can stand in the goal without my feet getting wet. So yeah, I'm feeling upbeat. But I don't want to get complacent. The Dynamos are a serious side. As soon as the whistle blows, I know it's gonna be tough.

Rex tries to perform one of his usual tricks—a rainbow flick—but a Delton player steals the ball away.

It's passed up the field at incredible speed, catching our defenders off-guard. Seconds later, I'm facing two unmarked Delton players who are hurtling their way towards me.

'Where's our defence?' I shout, trying to move forward to close down the attack. I can't mark both of the strikers. 'I need some help here!'

The words are barely out of my mouth before the inevitable happens. I've chosen to go at the guy with the ball, so all he has to do is pass to his teammate on the left who has a clear shot.

I do my best. I dive back to intercept, but I'm miles away and much too late as he fires the ball like a bullet from a gun into the back of the net. We're less than two minutes in and we're already losing.

I clamber to my feet, angry. 'Luke! Ashar! Where were you?'

'I was marking the other guy,' says Luke.

Ashar shrugs and turns away like it's not his problem.

Keep it together, Jed.

'It's alright, Jed. Don't worry.' Dave jogs over. 'It wasn't your fault.'

'I know it wasn't my fault,' I say, seething. 'But what's to stop it from happening again?'

'They took us by surprise, that's all. Trust me, we'll be fine.' He jogs back to his place in midfield.

I'm annoyed that he even *thinks* I might blame myself

for everyone else's mistake. And now I'm nervous as well. My stomach gurgles. I feel vulnerable back here by myself. I glance back at the net and it seems bigger than before. I'm much too small to reach the edges.

It was a stupid idea to play in goal. I don't know what got into me. There's no way I can do this.

I bounce up and down, trying to warm up and get my head back in the game.

Come on, Jed! Don't panic.

There are a few nerve-wracking minutes where possession keeps switching from one team to the other. Every time Delton have the ball, I feel tense. They're only a couple of passes away from their next shot.

And they're not messing about.

Their next attack is slower, but it's just as scary. They ease their way up the pitch using short passes to wrong-foot our defenders.

'Come on, Ashar!' I shout, frustrated as they slip past. If he messes up, it only puts more pressure on me.

Sure enough, the lanky striker finds some space and speeds towards the goal. This time, though, he has no-one to pass to. It's one on one.

I run forwards, desperate to close the angle and rush him into doing something stupid. But he's not daft. He lifts the ball into the air and over my head. I leap as high as

I can, but can't get anywhere close. As I fall to the ground, I twist around to see it land near the goal and bounce in. It seems to happen in slow motion.

Delton cheer and hug each other while I lay on the ground, pounding my fist in the mud. Two-nil, and it's not even close to half-time. We're getting smashed.

Worse still, when I get back to my feet and glance around, my teammates are giving me dark looks.

'Hey, don't blame me!' I shout. 'If anyone else wants to go in goal, then feel free!'

'No-one said anything, Jed,' points out Luke.

'You don't need to. I know what you're thinking.' I realise I sound like a crazy person, but I sense the pressure.

How does Miles deal with this every week?

I try to push it to the back of my mind, but my heart is thudding in my chest. My leg won't stop shaking, even when the action is in the other half.

Rex scores a blinder. That helps. For a moment there's hope. We could win!

But a few seconds later, Delton come at me again.

'Tackle him!' I shout, desperate for our useless defence to do something right. To be fair, Luke goes in hard and deflects the ball away, but that gives Delton a throw-in.

'Mark up,' calls Dave, sounding a lot calmer than me.

The defenders barely have time before the lanky guy

takes the throw, the ball sailing through the air a lot further than we expect. It finds the feet of one of the Delton midfielders, who quickly sends it on.

The problem is that our defenders are out of position, having moved to cover the throw-in, so it's down to me again.

What do I do?

As their winger comes towards me, I don't want to let him lob me again. But if I stand too far back, he'll shoot it past. All the confidence I had at training has now seeped away and I feel like a little kid. I edge forward, searching for the sweet spot between one mistake and the other.

Somehow, it works, more by luck than by skill.

As the attacker strikes the ball, trying to sneak it past me into the bottom corner, my leg shoots out at just the right moment and deflects it away.

'That's more like it!' shouts Brandon, grinning.

'Great reactions, Jed!' says Dave, slapping me on the back as we take our positions for the corner.

I'm glad I saved the shot, but I can't help feeling that if I let the next one in, they'll hate me again. I don't like this at all. I tug the turquoise socks as high as they'll go.

Everyone is in position, their breath visible in the cold air. It's quiet now as the Delton player lines up to take the corner.

He knows what he's doing. It's a perfect cross to one of his teammates, who's waiting by the box. I can see what's going to happen; a hard volley into the net.

Without thinking I dive towards the ball, clutching it to my chest as I land on the muddy ground. Seconds later, I feel a boot in my stomach as the striker follows through with his kick.

I know he didn't do it on purpose. I've almost done the same thing a hundred times myself. He was just going for the shot, and wasn't expecting me to get there before him.

But it still hurts.

There's the sound of a whistle. I hear the Delton player apologise. 'Sorry bro! Total accident!'

Sergeant Brillin runs over. 'Jed, Jed! Are you ok?'

I groan and sit up. 'Yeah, I think so.'

'Where did he kick you? Can I take a look?'

I lift up my shirt and the base layer top to show him a red mark where the boot made contact. 'He just winded me.'

'You're probably right. Sure you're up for playing on?' He reaches down to help me up.

'I am.' The only thing worse than being in goal would be to end up on the subs bench.

Once I'm on my feet, I slowly straighten my body and

take a few deep breaths. 'Come on. Let's get back to the game.'

***

The second half isn't any better than the first.

I watch, frustrated, as our players keep losing the ball to theirs. It's hard to see what we're doing wrong, but the game is a real slog. Our earlier enthusiasm has gone. Everyone is losing heart.

Everyone except the Delton Dynamos. For a while they pass between themselves, making our players do all the running. Once they've worn us out, they launch their next attack.

'Oh no,' I mutter, as three of them head towards the goal in a perfect V-formation. Ashar is heading to intercept them but Luke is some distance away.

This doesn't look good.

'I could use some help here!' I call out, sounding desperate.

I can call all I want. No-one comes. They nutmeg Ashar like he's asleep.

All it takes is one quick pass to the left, before they slide it into the goal. This time I don't dive. There's no point.

'You could at least try, Jed!' Luke's words sting as I head into the net to retrieve the ball.

'Me?' I shoot back. 'Where were you? Aren't you meant to be in defence?'

'I'm doing my best,' says Luke, looking hurt. 'I was marking the other forward.'

'The one that was nowhere near the goal?' I'm fuming now, my temper boiling over.

'Don't lay into him because you didn't save it.' Ashar is striding over, coming to Luke's defence.

'You can't talk! It's no surprise they got past you, is it? Your legs were so far apart they could have driven a bus through!'

Ashar shakes his head and turns away.

The rest of the team are watching, anxious. They know it won't end well if their goalie and defenders aren't getting on. And they're right.

By the time we slope off the pitch, we've lost 5-2.

I pull off the gloves and slam them down hard on the grass. 'I suppose you all think that was *my* fault.'

No-one says anything, but a few of them exchange glances, which only makes it worse.

'Well,' I carry on. 'I'd like to see any of you do better.'

'We're not blaming you,' says Dave, a little too late. 'It was a tough game and we could have *all* played better.'

Sergeant Brillin is standing behind him. 'Too right. And more to the point, we could have worked much better as a team. But we can sort that out tomorrow, can't we?'

'Tomorrow?' I glance up, confused.

'At the team-building day.'

'Oh yeah, right.' I'd forgotten all about that. When he'd first mentioned that, it sounded exciting. But right now, I don't want to spend another afternoon with this team.

And I doubt they want to spend it with me.

12. TEAMWORK

'Wear warm clothing.' That's what Sergeant Brillin said when he told us about the team-building day. 'You're gonna get muddy.'

Great, that's just what I need. More mud. Thanks, Coach.

I hunt through my wardrobe, looking for the best clothes to wear. It's not like I have loads to choose from. Half my stuff is dirty or hanging on the rack, still damp. I only have a few things left. One pair of ripped grey trackies, a thin sleeveless t-shirt and a too-small hoodie.

I can't live like this. We have to get our washing machine fixed.

The pile of stuff I wore in goal yesterday is heaped on the floor where I stripped it off. The Dynamos pitch was muddy, but not like our ground. I got dirty, but not drenched.

I couldn't, could I?

I try to decide what's worse: showing up in a dirty

football kit or the sleeveless t-shirt and trackies. I can hear the wind howling outside. There's no way my scratty t-shirt is going to be the right option. I'll freeze to death.

I reach down and pull the padded base layers from the pile. They're cold, but dry. I know they'll soon warm up if I pull them on. What choice do I have? I might as well go for it.

I tug it on; the turquoise strip as well as the skins. Then I look in the cracked mirror on my bedroom wall.

It's not too bad.

Well, it is. But I convince myself it'll be ok.

Before I can change my mind, I hear a horn beep. Dave's dad has pulled up outside in his old grey seven-seater. I don't want to keep him waiting.

I grab my water bottle and head out of the door, wondering what Sergeant Brillin has in store for us.

'Hey, Jed,' says Mr Hughes, as I climb in the back.

'Hi,' I reply. 'Thanks for giving me a lift.'

He always does, but that doesn't mean I take it for granted.

'No problem. Err, you know you're not playing football today, right?'

'I didn't have anything else to wear,' I admit. 'Our washing machine's busted.'

'Sorry to hear that. Can't it be fixed?'

'Dunno. Doubt it.'

'So, where are we going, Dad?' asks Dave. He's wearing waterproof trousers and a jacket, along with serious walking shoes, gloves and a woolly hat, making me feel totally under-prepared.

'I've told you, you'll see!' says Mr Hughes. 'Sergeant Brillin wants it to be a surprise.'

'Well, I hope it's a nice surprise,' says Dave. 'Like a team outing to eat pancakes.'

'In that case, you're in for a shock.' Mr Hughes looks at us through the rear-view mirror. 'You don't get muddy eating pancakes.'

He's right. I want to believe that this is some kind of jolly day out, but it all seems much more serious.

***

After what seems like an age, the car turns down a narrow track through some woods, and I jolt up and down as the suspension struggles with the bumpy terrain.

'Here we are.' Dave's dad pulls into a small clearing that seems to double as a car park. There are two other vehicles; Rex's BMW and Sergeant Brillin's hatchback.

A few of the lads are standing around, looking nervous. I'm relieved to see that Brandon is wearing a football kit as usual, so I won't be the only one. I'm kind of jealous because he has the latest Manchester City away kit. I'd die to have that, but given the grim surroundings, wearing white is probably a mistake.

Then someone else climbs out of Sergeant Brillin's car. But it can't be...

It's Miles!

I head over. 'Miles! You're back!' I shouldn't make a big deal out of it but I can't help myself.

He shrugs. 'Sort of. Sergeant Brillin chatted to my gran and convinced her this would be good for me. She was reluctant, but given that he's a police officer she let me come. Not that I *want* to be here.'

'Well, I'm glad you are. There's something I need to tell you. It's about the kids you're hanging out with.'

'Yeah? Well, I know you don't like them, so don't bother.'

'It's not that.' I grab his shoulders, eager to make him understand. 'I heard them chatting about you the other day, and they're leading you on. They're pretending to be your friends so you do their homework and stuff.'

Miles pulls away and narrows his eyes. 'Why should I believe you?'

'Because it's the truth,' I plead.

'Sure.' He folds his arms. 'Say what you want. I'm not

going to dump my friends just because they're a different crowd to you lot.'

This is gonna be harder than I thought. 'Don't you think it's odd they keep asking you for stuff? That you have to do their homework for them? And risk your neck to get their phone back from a teacher?'

Miles won't budge. 'It's not like that. We're mates, that's all. You do things for each other.'

'Yeah? Well what have *they* ever done for *you*?'

I can tell I've hit a nerve, but it makes him even more defensive. 'What have *you* ever done for me, Jed? You're no better than they are! You just want me to play in goal. At least they invite me to their houses.'

'Not all the time,' I point out. 'They only invite you when they want something.'

'Yeah, well *you* didn't even do that.'

I wonder if he's right. We've always relied on Miles to be our keeper, and he's always been there. Sometimes we'd laugh and joke at training, or even chill out together when our coach organised some event. But we've never done anything more.

I'm not sure what else to say, but Sergeant Brillin saves me the trouble. He calls us over.

'Right lads, I hope you're ready for a challenge?'

Some of the guys are enthusiastic, but I just shrug. I'm

thinking over my conversation with Miles, wondering if I can do anything to convince him his new friends are bad news.

Sergeant Brillin and Mr Hughes lead us down a short path to an area among the trees which is full of exciting-looking obstacles. Tyres hang over a muddy ditch. A scramble net covers part of the floor. There are various ropes, nets and logs spread around, creating a massive assault course.

'Wow, Coach, this looks awesome!' Brandon says what we're all thinking. Even I cheer up.

'We're going to split into teams of four,' says Sergeant Brillin, 'then see which team can complete the course the fastest.'

Brandon grabs my arm and pulls me towards Dave and Luke. Nothing can stop us when we're together. But I realise we're about to do what Miles accused us of. The four of us have got so close we've excluded the others. I look around me. When was the last time I spent time with Theo, or hung out with Rex? A couple of the lads are on the outside while me and my mates never have to worry. It shouldn't be like this.

'Guys,' I say. 'I'd love to be on a team with you but let's split up. Let's work with everyone else.'

Brandon looks at me like I've gone mad. 'You're not

serious? We're the dream team!'

'But the team is bigger than us four,' I point out. 'We already spend loads of time together. Let's mix it up.'

'Jed's right,' says Dave, glancing around. 'We need to get stuck in with the others. Besides, I already spend way too long with you losers.' He gives Brandon a playful shove.

'Fine,' Brandon grins. He can see it's an argument he's not going to win. 'But we'll soon see who the losers are around here. See you at the finish line!'

We break up and create chaos as we form new teams. I already know who I want in mine. I head straight over to Miles, who's standing with Harry and Kris. 'Can I join you?'

'Only if you shut up about my mates.'

'Deal.' I was hoping I'd get another chance to chat to him, but I'll settle for him not hating me.

'Right lads,' shouts Sergeant Brillin, 'there are a few health and safety pointers I have to let you know about...'

Rex groans. 'Do we have to, Coach?'

'Yeah, come on, Dad,' mutters Luke, embarrassed. 'We want to get going!'

'I know, I know.' Sergeant Brillin puts up his hands. 'But there are a couple of things I need to say. I'll be brief, I promise.'

It's not a promise he keeps. Our coach is a nice guy, but he sure knows how to talk. He's so careful to point out the dangers, I half expect him to warn us about snakes and crocodiles along with everything else.

By the time he's finished, we're desperate to get started.

'Right,' he says. 'Which team are going first?'

13. DITCH

'We—' I begin, but stop as Miles digs me in the ribs.

'Shh,' he warns.

I don't want to fall out with him again so I do as he asks and keep my mouth shut.

Brandon's team eagerly take their place at the starting line. He's with Rex, Theo and Ashar. They're a strong team; they'll probably win.

Sergeant Brillin blows his whistle and they shoot forwards, jumping on to the balance beams.

'Why didn't you want us to go first?' I mutter, now everyone is busy watching the action.

'Sometimes it's best to observe stuff,' says Miles. 'We'll get to see what works and doesn't work. On our turn, we won't make the same mistakes.'

I hadn't thought about that, but it kind of makes sense. We watch as Brandon attempts to cross the muddy ditch, using tyres swinging on long ropes. However hard he tries, he can't get his foot in the next one.

Miles mutters under his breath. 'He's making a mess of it. One of his teammates needs to get involved.' Rex and the others are focused on the next obstacle, instead of paying attention to Brandon's predicament.

Brandon is too proud to ask for help and tries to leap from one tyre to another. It doesn't go to plan. His foot slips, and he splats into the knee-deep mud.

As he staggers out of the ditch, dripping, everyone laughs.

Brandon can see the funny side, but he calls out to us. 'You won't be laughing when you try it! It's harder than it looks.'

His mum's not going to be laughing either when she sees the state of his kit.

'I hope I don't fall in that,' I say, shaking my head. The ditch doesn't just appear horrible, it smells grim too.

'Wrong attitude, Jed,' warns Miles. 'If you're scared, then you're more likely to fail.'

'So, I should *want* to end up in the ditch?'

'Sort of.' Miles sees I'm confused, so he presses on. 'By the time you've done the scramble nets over there, you're going to be filthy anyway, right? Chances are we're all gonna get mucky doing this. So, you might as well embrace it.'

'Easy for you to say,' I point out. 'You like getting

muddy.'

Miles snorts.

I look at him, surprised. 'Wait, are you saying you don't?'

'I used to hate it, Jed,' he says, quietly. 'I just wanted to play football so badly, and the only position that needed to be filled was the goalkeeper. Those first few games were tough. I was cold and dirty and I almost quit.'

'So why didn't you?'

'Because I love football. That's why. And I figured something out. If I changed my attitude, then it would be ok. So, I started looking forward to getting dirty. I made it like a personal challenge to see if I could get as muddy as possible.'

'Is that like reverse psychology or something?'

Miles shrugs. 'Probably. I dunno. But it worked. For me, at least.'

'So if we go into the assault course trying to get dirty, we'll enjoy it more?'

'Exactly.'

We stand in silence for a few minutes, watching the other teams.

Brandon's team have reached a high wall made of logs. Theo helps his teammates up by giving them a boost, but can't get up himself. The others have already jumped down and don't realise their mistake until it's too late. Now one of them has to climb back up from the other side to help him. It all takes time.

'They should have stayed on top and reached down to grab him,' mutters Miles. 'You can't get over that by yourself.'

Dave's team don't do any better. We watch as they try to cross the muddy ditch on a bridge that keeps twisting around under their feet, sending them crashing down into the muck.

'That's a tricky one,' admits Miles. 'Come on, we're next.'

We take our places at the starting line.

'Ready, boys?' asks Sergeant Brillin.

He blows his whistle and we dash forwards, over the balance beams. They're not too difficult, though the mud makes them slippery in places.

The tyres are much harder. You have to get a rhythm as a team, swinging forwards and backwards at the right time so you can connect with the next tyre in the line. Now we've seen Brandon's team make a mess of it, we have a much better idea of what to do, and we help each other across.

'Good work!' says Miles, taking the lead. Playing upfront I've never appreciated how much he does to keep the defence organised during a match, but after our last game I realise how badly we need him to give orders. 'To the wall!'

We follow him to the high obstacle.

'One of us needs to boost everyone else up. Jed, that's you.'

'Why me?' I ask, not sure if he's still mad at me.

'Because you're a skinny runt. When we have to lift you, it'll be a lot easier.'

'He's right,' agrees Kris. 'Hold out your hands.'

I cup my hands around his foot and use all my strength to boost him to the top of the wall. It's hard work, but only takes a couple of seconds before he gets a grip on the top and can pull himself up.

Then it's Harry's turn. He's heavier and I'm breaking a sweat by the time Miles takes his place.

We try the same thing again, but this time Miles can't reach the top. He's not as tall as the other two and my arms are too tired to lift him. After a few failed attempts, he drops back to the floor.

'Ok,' he says. 'Let me stand on your shoulders instead.'

I crouch down and he holds on to the wall as I slowly get to my feet with his feet either side of my head. Once I'm standing upright he can get a grip near the top and Harry helps to heave him up, while Kris leaps down the other side.

'Now it's your turn,' Miles shouts to me. 'Take a running jump and we'll grab you.'

'Sure.' I take a few paces back and run towards the wall.

If you've ever tried it, you'll know it's not easy. Your brain tells your body that you need to run but your body knows how much it's going to hurt if you hit that wall at full speed. As a result, my first attempt is half-hearted and I don't get high enough when I jump.

'Sorry,' I say, realising how feeble I'm being. 'I'll go again.'

'Hurry,' urges Miles. 'We're losing time.'

This time I have a better idea of when to jump and I time it perfectly. Miles and Harry grasp my hands and heave me to the top, my legs slipping and sliding on the logs as I'm lifted up.

Puffing and panting, I sit for a moment, relieved that we've done it. But this is no time for sitting around. We have to jump down the other side and press on.

More balance beams. Then a scramble net which we have to slide under on our bellies in the mud. Miles is right. It's a lot more fun if you decide you *want* to get dirty.

'This is awesome!' I say. Somehow, I'm enjoying

myself, even though I'm crawling through mud.

'That's the spirit! Come on, lads!' Miles climbs out from under the net, his front brown. He leads us over to the bendy bridge. Every other team has had to take several attempts at this. Each time someone is half-way across, the bridge twists sideways and hurls them down into the ditch below.

Brandon's team have finished and are watching from the sidelines, keen to see us suffer the same fate.

'Time to meet the ditch, lads,' shouts Theo, grinning. He's spent a fair amount of time in there himself, judging by his appearance.

I glance down at the knee-deep mud. 'We're doomed.'

'No, we're not.' Miles is firm. 'I've worked it out. There's only one way to do this. One of us stands in the ditch and holds the bridge steady.'

'You're serious?'

'Yeah, if you hold it right in the middle, it won't be able to twist around and the others can get across.'

'I'm not standing in that!' says Kris.

I can see his point. I can smell the stagnant mud from here.

'Someone has to,' says Miles, 'else we'll all be swimming in it, like the other team did.'

'Fine, I'll do it.' The words are out of my mouth

before I can stop myself.

'Really?' Miles looks shocked.

'Yeah. I *love* getting muddy, remember?' I give a brave smile, then take a running jump into the ditch, not even trying to cross the bridge. That way I can get at least half-way across.

As I land, the mud engulfs my legs up to my knees and splatters the rest of my body and face. I feel it oozing into my trainers, and seeping into my skins. It's freezing, and it smells disgusting.

I can see Brandon laughing out of the corner of my eye but I ignore him. I'm too busy grabbing the bridge with both hands, holding it tight.

'Ok,' I yell to the others. 'You can cross now.'

'One at a time,' warns Miles. 'That will be safest.'

They do as he says, each of our team members making their way over. The bridge is still wobbly, but not as unstable as it was for the others, and no-one falls in. I trudge to the other side of the ditch, brown from my thighs down.

'Will it count if I haven't crossed the bridge?' I ask, concerned.

'It has to,' says Miles. 'None of the other teams got *any* of their team members across it without falling in.'

From there, it's only a short distance to the finish line.

We race across, arm in arm, and everyone applauds.

'Well done, lads,' says Sergeant Brillin, looking pleased. 'You completed the course the fastest by far! Great teamwork!'

'Yeah?' I say. 'Well, we had a great leader.' I look over at Miles. He smiles.

'You stood in the ditch,' he points out.

'Yeah, well you know me. I'd do anything for a friend.'

14. ANSWERS

'Alright,' says Miles, as we trudge back to the cars, my trainers squelching. 'I'll tell you what's going on. You deserve to know.'

I'm surprised he's offered. I hadn't even asked. I didn't dare to mention it after his last outburst. 'If you're sure?'

He takes a deep breath. 'Mum had to go away on a business trip. All the way to New York.'

'Oh.' I can't imagine that. The furthest my mum has to travel for work is Welbeck.

'She sometimes has to do that,' he continues. 'Usually for one week a year. But this time she's had to stay for almost a month. While she's away, my gran looks after me.'

'What about your dad?' I ask.

'Dunno,' he says. 'Never met him.'

That's something we have in common.

How did I not know that?

'Sorry,' I say, awkwardly.

'Anyway, I spend loads of time on video games. Because I live in such a small village, there's not much else to do.'

'Tell me about it,' I agree.

'No, Jed.' Miles looks frustrated. 'You don't get it. You think Ferndale is a small village. But you have mates nearby and a football field and even a shop. You should try living in Thelham. There's nothing there, just some houses and farms. There's no-one else my age for miles.'

I hadn't thought about it before. Ferndale is small, but he's right out in the middle of nowhere. I try to play it down. 'You're only a few miles away from us. It's not that far. Dave and I biked it.'

'Yeah, *once*. You wouldn't want to make a habit of it, though, I bet.'

I decide to change the subject. 'So, you play loads of video games?'

'Yeah. Mum never let me play online, though. She already thought I was too addicted to screens and didn't like the idea of me connecting with strangers. But when she went away, I signed up to a month's free subscription for *Absolute War*.'

'And your gran let you?'

'She's clueless.' Miles grins at me. 'She knows nothing about technology. As far as she's concerned, I'm just playing games up in my room.'

'So how come you're grounded?'

'Well, I start playing online with these kids from school. You know who I'm on about. Rufus and his mates. And they're real friendly to me. They even invite me round to their houses for some tournaments. Gran's fine with it. She thinks I've got some friends at last.'

'But they're not real friends.' I can't stop myself saying it.

Miles sighs. 'They seemed ok at first. I felt like I could chill with them. But they needed help with stuff. Homework, mostly. They're not the brightest bunch.'

That's putting it mildly.

'So you offered to do it for them?'

'They pressured me into it. I thought I was being a good mate, but the more I did, the more they asked.'

'And your gran found out?'

'About the homework? No. But they asked me to meet up with them after school. We went shopping in the High Street. Gran thought I'd gone to football training.'

'What happened?' We stop walking for a moment. We're almost at the cars and I feel like I'm about to get some answers. I can't bear the idea that someone might interrupt.

'They're always teasing me that I'm this goody-two-shoes kid who's too afraid to do anything bad.' Miles looks away, into the woods. 'They dared me to steal a new game from the store. They said if I did it, I'd properly be in their crew.'

Now I understand. 'You got caught?'

'It was the worst moment of my life. The security guard stopped me and called the police and everything. The others had scarpered by then, of course. Sergeant Brillin showed up and he couldn't believe it when he saw me. I nearly died of embarrassment.'

Now it makes sense. Sergeant Brillin knew more than he was letting on, but he didn't want to embarrass Miles.

'So that's why your gran grounded you?'

'Yeah. And she guessed other kids were involved. She thought I'd gone into town after football practice, so assumed it was you lot I was hanging out with.'

'That's why she had a go at me and Dave.'

Miles nods. 'Sorry about that.'

'But you kept meeting up with Rufus and his crew?'

'Only online. Gran had no idea I was even doing it or she'd have gone mad. But there was no-one else to talk to. I know it sounds crazy, but I get so lonely out in that village. They let me chill with them at school as well and I felt like I finally had some real friends.'

'But they made you graffiti a wall?'

'It was a challenge. I couldn't say no. They'd never let me hang out with them if they thought I was too scared to do it. And then Rufus needed his phone back, and asked me to get it.'

'Miles, you know this is messed up, right? Real friends don't make you do stuff like that.'

Tears form in his eyes. 'It all happened bit by bit. I was in too deep and I couldn't say no.'

'And you were too busy doing their homework to do your own?'

He nods miserably. 'Doing their homework and playing *Absolute War*.'

'I'm sorry, Miles.'

'It's not your fault,' he sniffs.

'But it is my fault,' I insist. 'It's all of our fault. Me. Dave. Brandon. Luke. We spend so much time together we don't think about anyone else on the team. But that's gonna change.'

Miles looks up at me. 'What do you mean?'

'You're invited to our next sleepover. The next one that you're allowed to come to, anyway.'

'Probably in three years time,' he mutters. 'Mum's gonna go mental when she gets back and finds out what's been happening. Gran hasn't said anything over the phone because she didn't want to worry her.'

I feel for him. I really do. 'Look, mate. There's only one thing you can do now. Tell the truth. Trust me. I've been in a similar situation. If you lie about it, you just get deeper and deeper. Tell your gran what happened. And your mum when she's back.'

'I'm so dead.' Miles wipes his eyes with his muddy sleeve. 'She'll take away my games.'

'Probably.' I shrug. 'But you'll get them back, eventually. And you'll feel a lot better.'

He doesn't object. He knows what I'm saying makes sense.

'Besides,' I add. 'You know what you can do instead?'

'What?' he says, confused.

'Play more football.' I grin at him and he gives me a playful push.

'You sure all this talk of sleepovers and owning up to my gran isn't because you want your keeper back?'

'No, Miles,' I reply. 'Even if you never play in goal again, I still want you as a mate.'

And it's true. Much as I'd love him back between the posts so I can return to playing up front, I care more about his feelings than our need for a goalie.

'Thanks, Jed.'

We bump fists and start making our way towards the cars. Several of the lads have stripped off the worst of their muddy clothing and are drying themselves with towels. Some of them have brought some spare clothes in a bag like Sergeant Brillin told us to.

I look at Mr Hughes apologetically. 'I didn't bring any spare clothes.'

He rubs his forehead in despair. 'Oh, Jed. Well you might have to travel on the roof-rack then!'

I smile. 'If you like.'

'Just get the worst stuff off and we'll have to manage.'

I strip off my clothes, until I'm only wearing the base layer tights, then scramble on to the back seat.

As Dave's dad starts the engine and we drive off, I see Miles standing by Sergeant Brillin's hatchback.

He smiles at me and waves as we go past.

I finally know what's going on.

And it feels good.

15. RELIEF

I might have solved one problem, but my life is far from sorted.

There's still some graffiti on the wall, and on Monday I'm back at it, trying to get it clean. I've only managed to remove a few of the letters, even though I'm scrubbing hard.

'Jed.' The voice makes me jump. I turn around to find Mr Grierson standing right behind me. I wish he'd stop sneaking up on me like that.

'Yes, sir?' I wonder if I'm in trouble for something else.

'Looks like you've been working hard at this.' He examines the wall. 'Not easy getting it off, is it?'

'No, sir.' I imagine he's here to give me another lecture.

'All of our mistakes are like that, lad.' He gives me a long, hard look. 'They're easy to make, and really hard to clear up.'

There's a pause, like he's waiting for a response.

'Yes, sir.'

'But I think you've learned your lesson, this time at least. The school caretaker will take things from here.'

I can hardly believe my luck. 'You mean...?'

'Yes, you can go. Get out of my sight before I change my mind.'

I back away. 'Yes, sir. And, err, thanks, sir.'

I dash off before he decides he's been too lenient, glad to be free.

***

I don't escape rugby that easily.

I'm back in the changing room after school on Wednesday. I haven't even started getting my kit on before Tristan sidles over.

'My new training partner,' he mocks. 'Looking forward to another *long* session.'

The truth is I've been dreading it all week, but I'm not going to admit that. 'Sure. Last week was fun.'

He looks a little surprised. 'Well, don't expect me to go so easy on you this time.'

I feel panic rising inside. Hopefully, he's just winding me up.

I cheer up as I reach into my bag and pull out the

goalkeeper skins Brandon gave me. With this much padding, I'm hoping I don't feel anything, not even the cold.

There's one more thing that's going to make a difference this time when I play. I remember what Miles said to me about how he used to hate getting dirty, but when he changed his attitude, it was fun. So, today I've decided I'm gonna get properly muddy.

And I'm gonna enjoy it.

Tristan pairs up with me like before for the opening drills.

I keep smiling and throw myself into it. 'Challenge you to get me in the puddle again,' I grin, as I face him down.

He's confused. 'If you insist.'

As I run towards him, he edges me to the corner of the rectangle, just like before. But this time I'm not trying to avoid the mud. I drive on straight through it.

To give him credit, he only hesitates for the briefest moment before he hurls himself at my waist and we both tumble into the puddle.

'This is so much fun,' I say, clambering to my feet, cold and wet. I offer him my hand. He refuses it as he stands up, dripping.

'Huh.' He stalks off to take his place on the line.

But from that moment on, something changes.

Partly because of my change of attitude, and partly because of the padded skins, I'm starting to enjoy this.

The more Tristan tackles me, the more fun I have. I get a few bumps and scratches, but it's nothing like the crushing I had last week.

And when at the end of the session, Mr Davidson tells us we have a match on Friday, I find myself looking forward to it.

'I have to admit, Jed, I wasn't sure whether you'd stick this out,' says the teacher, as we walk back to the changing room. 'I thought you'd quit. But you really got stuck in today.'

'Yes, sir. It was fun.'

I'm not even lying. When you approach it with the right attitude, it turns out rugby isn't so bad.

Who knew?

***

By the following Saturday, there's an enormous pile of dirty laundry in the corner of my room which I'm going to have to tackle at some point this weekend.

As I'm getting ready for football, I get a text from Luke which cheers me up. 'You don't need to wear your goalie stuff today. Miles is coming.'

I collapse on the bed in relief.

Finally.

We have our goalie back!

I wonder what he said to his gran, so she'd let him play. Did he tell her everything or only some of it?

Either way, it's good news.

I don't have to spend another match with the team getting annoyed at me every time I make a mistake.

The other reason it's a huge relief is that my goalie kit still hasn't recovered from the assault course.

I tried to wash it, but the smell of that ditch didn't ever properly come out. There are some jobs you can't do by hand.

That meant I would have been in the luminous yellow kit today, and I didn't want to wear that in public. Instead, I can pull on my orange Foxes strip and take my place as a striker where I belong.

When I get to the field, I see the lads gathered round. In the middle is Miles, looking confident.

The minute we play, you can tell the difference.

Our defenders know what they're doing as Miles shouts out instructions. He warns them of danger, encourages them whenever they do something right. He's always watching, reading the game, trying to work out what the other team are up to and where they're going wrong. Just like he did on the assault course.

Meanwhile, now I'm back up front, the Foxes play their best. There's a natural chemistry between Brandon, Rex and me that works. There's no stopping us.

I fire the ball into the goal for the third time before the half-time whistle blows. It's 3-0 and we're owning the opposition.

'It's good to have you back,' I say to Miles, as we swig our drinks.

'It's good to be back. I did what you said. I told my gran everything. She took away my games, but said I could start playing football again. Especially if Sergeant Brillin is here to keep an eye on me.'

'Will she let you come to a sleepover?'

'Not yet.'

'Well, let us know as soon as you can.'

Dave suddenly pulls a face and glances behind me. He's seen something that scares him, and I turn around to check it out.

Miles' gran is standing there. I remember what she said about never wanting to see me again. I step back and prepare myself for a verbal caning, but it turns out that's not why she's here.

'I owe you an apology, young man,' she says, kindly. 'I accused you of getting Miles into trouble, but you were trying to be a good friend. Both of you were.' She turns to Dave as well. 'I hope you'll forgive me. I was worried about him.'

'Sure,' I say, a little embarrassed. 'No worries. I get why you thought it was us.'

'Yeah,' says Dave. 'We're just glad Miles is back on the team.'

'Once Miles can see his friends again, you'll have to come around for tea and cakes.'

I almost burst out laughing and Miles turns bright red, but he doesn't need to worry. Dave has it under control.

'That would be really nice,' he says, warmly. 'We look forward to it.'

She wanders off, looking pleased.

Even I feel warm inside. I'm not used to people saying sorry to me. Especially adults.

'Well, that's a good sign,' mutters Miles. 'Maybe I'll be able to come to a sleepover sooner than I think.'

I clap him on the back. 'I hope so. Someone has to beat Brandon at FIFA. That boy is way too good.'

Miles grins. 'I reckon I could manage that.'

16. WASHING

So, now it's just me and the washing.

It sits there in the corner, like a monster that's growing every day. Maybe it will come alive while I'm asleep and attack me? Ok, so that's not going to happen. But neither will it wash itself. At some point I'm gonna be spending some serious time at the sink.

I can't put it off much longer. After my post-match shower, I'm down to my last set of clothes. It's a good job tight-fitting trackies are in fashion, because these are way too small. They also ride up my shins revealing my not-very-white socks. I decide to tuck the trackies into them, so it looks deliberate.

No way am I gonna deal with the pile of washing right now. First, I'm heading to Dave's for some serious downtime, before Mum gets back.

Dave's used to me looking scruffy, but even he does a second take as I walk into his house. 'If you don't mind me saying, Jed,' he says, as diplomatically as he can, 'you're looking especially chavvy today.'

Brandon is standing on the stairs. 'Yeah, mate. What's happening with those trackies?'

'Shut it, both of you.' I'm not mad at them. I'd say the same if one of them showed up looking like this. 'I'm running out of clothes. We're a bit behind on the washing.'

'So are we,' says Brandon. 'I had to wear my Coventry strip today.'

I hadn't realised there were some he preferred. 'Poor you,' I say, sarcastically. 'But I bet you still have some other clean clothes in that vast wardrobe of yours.'

Brandon shrugs. 'Fair point.'

As we head up into Dave's room, a question pops into my head and I turn to Brandon. 'Why on earth is your mum behind on the washing? Isn't she obsessed with doing it?'

'Usually,' he says. 'But since we got a new kitchen, she's not been able to. They're waiting for the new washing machine to get here.'

'What's wrong with the old one? Did it break?'

'Nah. It's white,' he says matter-of-factly, as if that makes any sense.

'Err, Brandon, aren't all washing machines white?' I ask, feeling like I'm stating the obvious.

'Mum wants a silver one to match the fridge and the cooker.'

'Right.' It takes a moment for that to sink in. Brandon lives in a different world to me. I couldn't imagine ever throwing out a perfectly good washing machine just because it was the wrong colour.

A perfectly good washing machine...

Wait a minute!

'Brandon, what's happening with your old one?' I ask, sounding crazy now, like the only kid in the world who's interested in household appliances. 'Is she selling it?'

'I don't think so.' Brandon shrugs. 'She hates selling stuff second-hand. Too much hassle. I think they're gonna take it down the tip.'

I want to grab him and shake him hard by the shoulders. 'Err, do you think we could have it, maybe?' I sound desperate, but I *need* that washing machine.

'Sure, I guess. But how will you get it to your house?'

That's not an easy question to answer.

Dave looks up. 'Dad might help.'

Mr Hughes to the rescue again!

'That would be amazing,' I say. 'Can we ask him? Like, right now?'

'Really, Jed, right now?' Dave is confused at my sudden interest in Brandon's trash.

'Yeah, bro,' cuts in Brandon. 'Wouldn't you rather play FIFA?'

I want to knock their stupid heads together. 'Yes, I'd RATHER play FIFA!' I explode. 'Of course I would! But we don't have a working washing machine at home so if I don't sort it then I'm either gonna spend most of my childhood wearing dirty clothes or plunging my pants into the sink by hand. Is that what you want? Is it?'

'Seriously?' Dave looks shocked. 'I didn't realise it was that bad.'

'Chill, bro.' Brandon puts his hand on my shoulder. 'If it's that important to you then I'll call my mum right now.'

'And I'll see if my dad can help shift it,' says Dave. 'Let's do this!'

***

The assault course was a great way for us to practice working together as a team. But shifting a washing machine is even better.

They're heavy. Like really heavy.

It takes all of us with Dave and Brandon's dads to lift it into the back of the car and only just fits when all the seats are down.

'Where are you taking it?' asks Brandon's dad. I can tell he wants to get back to whatever he was doing, but he can see that Mr Hughes is going to need help at the other end.

'Across the village, to Jed's place.'

Brandon's dad considers it for a moment, glancing over at me in my too-short trackies. He must decide I'm a worthy cause. 'I'll come and give you a hand.'

I'm not too keen on all these people seeing inside my place. The outside is bad enough. Normally they don't get past the front garden. But what can I do? Right now, I need their help. We have to get the old washing machine out of the kitchen and the new one in, and that's gonna take everyone.

I lead them through the hallway, embarrassed at the bare floorboards and peeling wallpaper. None of them say anything. They're too polite.

When I get into the kitchen, I wish I'd made more of an effort to clean up. If Brandon's mum thought their old kitchen was bad, she'd die of shock if she ever came here.

'That's the old one,' I say, pointing to the useless hunk of metal in the corner.

'What should we do with it?' asks Mr Hughes, as he looks at the broken machine. 'I'd take it down to the tip, but it'll be shut by now.'

'Just leave it in the front garden,' I suggest. 'We'll sort it later.'

We won't. There's already an old washing machine there which has been there for years, so there's no way we'll ever get rid of this one either. But our garden's a dumping ground. What difference will it make?

'If you're sure.' Mr Hughes doesn't look too happy with the idea, but he can't see any alternative. Puffing and panting, we edge the washer out and dump it on the knee-high grass before hauling the new one through.

Mr Hughes knows how to connect all the pipes. 'There you go, Jed,' he says. 'All set up.'

'Thank you so much. Mum's gonna be over the moon.' Truthfully, so am I. I haven't been this happy since I got given an old Playstation last Christmas. How sad does that make me? But if you had to wash all your clothes by hand, you'd understand.

'Glad we could help,' says Mr Hughes.

Brandon's dad is already backing out of the house. 'Thanks for taking it off our hands.'

Dave and Brandon are standing in the corner, not sure what to say. I can tell what they're thinking. My house is nothing compared to theirs. I wonder if they'll still want to be my friends now they've seen how I live.

'It's a bit of a dump,' I say, trying to save them the

trouble.

Brandon shrugs. 'It's a kitchen. Who cares? Now, can we *finally* play some FIFA?'

***

Brandon wins every game.

Normally I'd find that annoying, but today I don't care.

Luke's joined us, and the four of us are having a great time. I realise how lucky I am to have friends like these. I wonder how long it will be before Miles can come as well.

'I think we should invite other people to our gaming sessions,' I say after a while. 'As well as Miles, I mean.'

'We only have four controllers,' points out Luke.

'So, we take it in turns,' I suggest. 'We need to spend more time with the others. I don't want any of the team feeling left out.'

'I agree,' says Dave.

'Maybe we could do winner stays on?' says Brandon. 'That way I get to play all the time!'

I glance at Luke and he looks over to Dave. We don't hear what Brandon says next, because the three of us pile on top of him and start beating him with pillows.

'Do you think he's had enough?' says Luke, after a few

minutes.

I'm about to answer, but Brandon interrupts. 'I dunno, Luke. Have you had enough of losing eight-nil?'

The play-fight continues, the four of us rolling around like a pack of animals until we collapse on the floor exhausted.

'I better go,' I say, looking at the time. 'Mum will be back from work soon and I want to see her face when she gets home.'

***

I make it just in time.

Mum lights up like a Christmas tree when she sees the new washing machine. 'Is that...? How did you...?' She can't finish any of her questions.

'Sit down, Mum. I'll make some tea.'

'But, Jed, that looks brand new! We can't afford it!'

'Brandon's mum was chucking it out,' I explain, filling up the kettle. 'It was the wrong colour. Dave and Brandon's dads helped me get it here.'

'The wrong colour?' Mum's having trouble taking it all in.

'Apparently so. Turns out that all the trendy people have silver ones.' I press down the switch and turn towards her. 'So, I hope you don't mind that it's white?'

'I think we'll manage.' She bursts out laughing and pulls me into a hug. 'You're a good boy, Jed. I don't know what I'd do without you.'

'Well, for one thing,' I say, smiling up at her. 'You'd have to make your own tea.'

'There is that,' she agrees. 'How was the match today?'

'It was amazing. We won five-nil. I scored two of them.'

'Good lad! So, you didn't have to play in goal?'

'No. Miles is back. And I know one thing for sure. I'm never gonna take him for granted ever again.'

And I mean it. I've well and truly learned my lesson.

Not only will I appreciate everything Miles puts up with as our keeper.

I'll also look out for him as a friend.

A NOTE FROM THE AUTHOR

Thanks for reading 'The Grounded Goalie'.

I hope you enjoyed it, and you're looking forward to hearing more stories about Jed and the Ferndale Foxes. If you haven't read them yet, then make sure you get hold of the other books in the series. They're full of action, suspense and... you guessed it... football!

Meanwhile, you can connect with my readers' club at:

www.subscribepage.com/footballkids

If you're under thirteen, your parents will need to sign up for you. I'll keep you informed of any new releases, as well as giving you opportunities to get freebies, prizes and giveaways. Best of all, there's the opportunity to send me football photos to try to win a place on one of my book covers!

Also, check out my Instagram @zacmarksauthor where I post football forfeit challenges, where kids sometimes end up egged or with boots full of shaving foam! Check it out and get your parents to message me if you want a challenge of your own!

Finally, it would be a huge help to me if you would get your parents to post a review on Amazon for this book. Could you do that? I promise I read every review!

Stay connected – I love hearing from my readers, and who knows, maybe you or your team could make it into one of Jed's adventures!

Thanks so much for being a part of my story.

Zac.

THE CRAFTY COACH

The Ferndale Foxes are in trouble. With no coach, the team will fold.

Jed needs to act fast! He can't imagine life without football. But saving the team is going to be tough: he has to find a way to turn things around, both on and off the pitch.

There's one person who might be able to coach them, but he isn't the kind of person you'd usually ask. Will he be a great choice or will it end in disaster?

Jed has some tough decisions to make, the kind you shouldn't have to make at twelve; the kind that can get you into trouble! Just how far will he go in his attempts to rescue the team? And will it all be worth it in the end?

'THE CRAFTY COACH' is the first book in the 'Football Boys' series: action-packed books for football and soccer-mad kids aged 9-13. It's available now on Amazon!

THE SNEAKY SUB

It's no fun being on the bench. Jed's finding out the hard way.

Someone isn't playing fair. Jed and his mates are competing for places on the team, but one of his teammates will do anything to keep him off the pitch.

The problem is, he doesn't know who.

He has to solve the mystery, and fast! They're making his life a total misery and they'll stop at nothing to get a game.

But how is he going to find out who's responsible? And what action should he take?

One thing's for sure: at twelve, you have enough to deal with, without being hassled by a Sneaky Sub!

'THE SNEAKY SUB' is the second book of the 'Football Boys' series: action-packed books for football and soccer-mad kids aged 9-13. It's available now on Amazon!

THE TERRIBLE TOURNAMENT

It should be the best summer ever. But it's the worst!

When the Ferndale Foxes head off for a football tournament by the sea, they have no idea how tough it will be.

Jed and his teammates can't catch a break, and everything seems to go wrong. Faced with one problem after another, the team falls apart.

It's not easy to stay friends when you feel like a loser.

Will they be able to turn it around before it's too late?

'THE TERRIBLE TOURNAMENT' is the fourth book in the 'Football Boys' series: action-packed books for football and soccer-mad kids aged 9-13. It's available now on Amazon!

DO YOU LOVE FOOTBALL?

Aged 9-13?

Do you eat, sleep and breathe football?

Would you like to take on a challenge?

Want to win some new kit or free books?

Or even appear on a book cover?

Visit www.subscribepage.com/footballkids for information on all this and more!